The Auberon Witches

Destiny Series

TARA WEEKS

TARA WEEKS
NEWSLETTER

Sign up for my Paranormal Women's Fiction newsletter on Facebook and get Free Book Updates, Giveaways and Book Promotion Specials!

@taraweeksauthor.com

"And above all, watch with glittering eyes the whole world around you because the greatest secrets are always hidden in the most unlikely places. Those who don't believe in magic will never find it."

— Roald Dahl

CONTENTS

Destiny In Danger

Destiny Revealed

Destiny Forever

Introduction

A paranormal women's fiction series.

Adamina's life was turned upside down when her husband confessed to an affair with a younger colleague—who also happened to be pregnant with his child. She had longed for children for as long as she could remember, but instead, Addie finds herself on her fortieth birthday more alone than ever.

Rich and sheltered Selene underwent a life-changing epiphany after a health scare which opened Selene's eyes to the gilded cage she had spent her life in. Realizing she has no love for the husband she has been forced to marry, or the life that they lead, she decides to celebrate her fortieth birthday by fleeing everything she's ever known.

Cassiopeia's grief has enveloped her in a dark cocoon of sadness after the deaths of her husband and two children. Yet she decides that, at forty, she still has a life to live, and she wants to honor their memory by living it to the fullest.

Never underestimate the hand of fate…

Destiny Awaits

Chapter One

Adamina Naya sat at her dressing table, examining the reflection of her tear-stained face. It was her fortieth birthday and yet, as she turned her face from one side to the next, Addie tried to convince herself she didn't look it. Not that she really knew what forty was supposed to look like. She attributed her youthful appearance to her alabaster skin—a curse in her youth when all she wanted was a sun-kissed tan like her friends. But as she aged, she realized it was a blessing. Her deep copper hair fell in waves around her face and hovered just above her shoulders, and her deep blue eyes were bloodshot and puffy.

Happy Birthday.

Addie had never felt so alone. Biting her lower lip, she tried to hold back the tears that threatened to start up again, instead distracting herself by pinning her hair back at the temples with bobby pins. Her engagement ring glinted as the light from the dresser hit it, and Addie lowered her hands as she stared at it. Over 15 years she had worn it with pride and joy. Now it only brought her pain and misery. Twisting it this way and that, Addie eventually pried both her engagement and wedding rings from her finger and tossed them into her modest jewelry box, closing the lid on them for good.

Addie tried to push her thoughts away as she tapped the screen on her phone to check the time. Her husband, Luka—or soon to be ex-husband—would arrive in an hour to take her out for a birthday dinner. It was the last thing she wanted to do, but Luka was adamant he wanted them to stay on friendly terms, despite the fact he had cheated on her and left her for a younger woman. Each of her attempts to decline his invitation had been ignored as he had continued to send her confirmations and reminders. Addie could hardly believe the nerve of him. First, he announced he was leaving her—completely out of the blue, or so Addie had thought—and then he insisted on celebrating her birthday with her…and to add insult to injury, she had recently learned that Luka's new love was pregnant.

Addie gripped the edge of the dressing table as yet another panic attack threatened to engulf her, and as she struggled to control her breathing, she tried to focus on anything other than Luka.

Suddenly, a vision of green trees flashed before her. Not just any trees, but great big looming ones, the kind that filled old forests and you knew just by looking at them, that they had been there longer than any living person on the planet. Almost instantly, Addie felt a calm sweep over her, and her panic attack subsided. She knew the cause. It wasn't because he had left her. Or even that he had left her for someone younger. Not entirely, anyway. It was because he was finally going to become a father. It was a dream they had shared since they had first started dating, of surrounding themselves with children and leading a boisterous and crazy, but love-filled life. Only it never happened. It turned out that Addie couldn't have children and, despite the promises and assurances that he loved her no matter what, she always suspected that it would come to this. The allure of fatherhood was too strong.

Taking a deep, shaky breath, Addie gently dabbed at her eyes, trying to keep her makeup in place, and as the sound of a car horn emanated from outside the house, she rose from the dressing table and gathered her suitcase and bags. At the bedroom door, she turned for one last look at the bed she had shared with her husband for all those years. Weighed down in her sadness, Addie closed the door behind her, leaving her wedding ring and memories behind her.

Addie opened the front door, and without a backwards glance, walked down the short path to where the Uber driver stood waiting. She returned his friendly greeting with as much faux friendliness as she could muster, and sliding into the back seat, Addie directed the driver to the airport.

* * *

Cassiopeia Zephyr traced the faces in the photograph with her finger. She had found a calming comfort in the repetitive exercise and yet it did nothing to fill the aching void in her heart. Having tucked the photo safely into her suitcase, she hesitated before zipping it up. She had already reopened it three times. Spotting her phone charger sitting on the bedside table, Cassie walked towards it, when it suddenly fell to the ground. She stopped, staring down at where it now lay on the carpet. She slowly crouched down, her fingers running over the cord as she let herself toy with the idea that maybe it was one of her children trying to get her attention. It was a comforting thought as Cassie scooped it up and got to her feet. Closing the suitcase, she dragged it from her room and down the stairs to the front door. She checked her watch, and seeing that she still had some time before her brother arrived to take her to the airport, she decided to take a walk through the house one last time.

Stepping into the lounge room, her hands shoved into the pockets of her navy slacks, she could still see her children, Shep and Olive, playing board games together on the carpet, and her husband, Harley, smiling at them over the newspaper he was reading in his favorite chair. Swallowing the lump rising in her throat, Cassie walked through the living room into the kitchen. Placing her hands palm down on the immaculate island bench, she could see her family sitting on the stools opposite her, Shep and Olive pleading with her to make them pancakes for breakfast as she poured them both some cereal before school, Harley promising to make them pancakes at the weekend. Each room was filled with memories; memories of a life spent with a family she no longer had. At first the memories had felt comforting, but now it was torment to be surrounded by them. Cassie felt as if she was drowning. Back at the front door, she checked her reflection in the large oval mirror that hung on the wall. It had been a wedding present, though it was so long ago now, she couldn't recall who from. Flipping her long, sandy blonde hair over her shoulders, she tucked what she could of her side fringe behind her right ear. Her large green eyes stared back at her, as though she was looking at a stranger. Cassie thought her slender face looked harrowed from her grief and she wondered if she would be able to smile again, even if she wanted to. She took a step back to get a better look at her overall appearance. Cassie wasn't superficial in the sense that she had to be done up to go anywhere, but she was pedantic about neatness. Smoothing down the imagined creases in her cream blouse and navy slacks, she sighed at what she considered to be a rather boyish figure. Cassie had always been slim—she didn't think her weight had changed much at all since high school—but she had always longed for some womanly curves.

With a sigh, Cassie opened the front door and dragged her bags outside to wait for her brother to take her to the airport.

* * *

Selene Beaufort tapped her Jimmy Choo impatiently against the marble floor of the foyer as she watched the staff carry her bags down the stairs, the sound of her husband's voice in her ear like the annoying buzzing of a mosquito that wouldn't go away.

"Selene, please, you're being ridiculous. One little thing happens that doesn't fit in with your idea of what your life should be, and you just decide to throw it all away," Edward said; Selene wondered if his voice had always had that whiny sound to it, or if it was a recent development.

"Take them straight out to the car." Selene directed the staff as they hurried past her.

"That's mature, Selene. You're just going to ignore me like some obstinate child!" her husband declared.

"There's a difference between obstinance and apathy, Edward," Selene replied with a sigh as her handbag vibrated against her side and she reached into the side pocket and withdrew her mobile. With an inward groan Selene saw it was her mother calling. Again. After six unanswered calls from her father—he had obviously passed the torch onto her mother. Selene tossed the phone back into her bag.

"Aren't you going to answer that? It's rude not to answer your phone. Your parents are worried sick about you. We all are," her husband rambled; Selene was unable to stop herself from rolling her eyes. Of course he had gone running to her parents to get them involved, hoping that with a quick, stern talking to, she would return to her husband with her tail between her legs, pleading for his forgiveness. She was saddened because 12 months ago, that's exactly what would have happened—not that she would have been brave enough to act this way then anyway. Selene couldn't wait to get away from all of them.

Doing her best to tune her husband out, she walked over to the enormous mirror hanging on the left wall of the foyer and inspected her impeccable makeup. She pulled a small tub of expensive tinted lip gloss from her bag and unscrewed the lid. With her newly ringless ring finger, she dabbed at the lip gloss and tapped the dusky pink across her plump lips. Rubbing them together, she lifted her head to the side, trying to determine if the lip gloss helped soften her features at all. Selene had always had high cheekbones, much to the envy of her friends. The downside was, if she was ever stressed or unwell, they became too pronounced, causing her to look gaunt. As an afterthought, Selene dipped her finger back into the lip gloss and rubbed it into her cheeks, trying to give her face some color. Her waist-long chestnut hair was perfectly blow-dried and kept away from her face with a pair of antique combs that had belonged to her grandmother.

"Mrs. Culpepper, the car is packed and ready," came the nervous voice of the servant hovering behind her.

"It's Beaufort. Ms. Beaufort," Selene stated as she turned around.

"Really Selene? Beaufort? You can't just revert back to your maiden name…"

"Of course I can," Selene replied, cutting her husband off. She walked over and gave him an emotionless kiss on the cheek before following the servant out to the car, leaving him dumbfounded and staring after her. Without a single look back at the mansion that she now viewed as her gilded cage, she stepped down the path to the waiting limousine and slid elegantly into the back. As the door was closed after her, Selene reached over to the mini bar and poured herself a glass of champagne, not caring that it was still morning. Raising her glass, she toasted her newfound freedom.

Chapter Two

Addie

Addie stared up at the flight board in dismay as one flight after another was either delayed or cancelled. An unseasonal storm had seemingly come out of nowhere and was wreaking havoc across half the country. It was so loud; she could hear it whistling over the roof of the terminal. She glanced down at her phone ringing in her hand and saw it was Luka. Again. Addie allowed herself a small smile of satisfaction, knowing he would be outraged that she had stood him up.

Suck it, you son of a bitch.

Looking back up at the board, Addie groaned as she saw that her flight was cancelled. She looked around, wondering what to do now. The last thing she wanted was to go home and sheepishly have to face her smug ex.

Addie made her way over to the staff at the closest gate, deciding she would get on any flight she could. It didn't really matter where she went, just so long as she was as far away from her life as possible.

Before she could reach the desk, a woman barreled into her before apologizing profusely. Addie grabbed hold of the woman's arm while she steadied herself. Instantly, Addie could feel the woman's sadness, her listlessness. It felt like she was getting a sneak peek into the stranger's soul; the sensation was so strange that she quickly released her.

"Are you okay?" she asked.

The woman looked at her for the first time, and Addie noticed that, while she was very beautiful, she seemed a little out of place. And she appeared to have been drinking as she teetered on her stilettos. Addie felt frumpy next to the tall, slim elegance of the woman beside her, and self-consciously smoothed down her dress.

"Ah, I don't know. I'm supposed to get on a plane, but they said I can't. Something about the weather. It was sunny before, wasn't it?" she asked distractedly.

"Um, it was a little overcast at my place, but certainly didn't look like a storm was coming, that's for sure." Addie replied.

"I just need to get on the plane. Can you please point me in the right direction?" the woman asked. It was then that Addie realized the stranger had no idea what she was doing, which seemed amazing to her. She held her hand out, "I'm Adamina Naya. My friends call me Addie."

The woman flashed her a charming smile and held her own hand out. "I'm Selene Cul…Beaufort." There was a brief zap as their hands touched and they quickly let go.

"Ouch! You zapped me!" Selene exclaimed, shaking her hand and staring at Addie as though she had intentionally done so.

"There must be increased static in the air with the storm. Come on, let's go see what we can do about getting on any remaining flights," Addie instructed, and tentatively led the way. Selene followed, looking relieved to have someone take control.

As they approached the rapidly growing line at the help desk, two young guys barged in front of them, knocking Selene's handbag from her grasp and sending its contents across the carpet. They insincerely apologized before turning their backs on the women, with no intention of picking up the bag and its contents. Addie got down onto the ground as Selene feigned an attempt, "Oh, well since you're already picking them up..."

Who is this woman and what planet is she from?

"Here you go," said a friendly voice, attached to an extended hand containing a Dolce & Gabbana lipstick and a Versace glasses case. Addie looked up with a grateful smile as she took the items and dumped them into the handbag. Getting to her feet, she held it out to Selene, who absently took it without thanks as she scanned the length of the queue before them. Addie rolled her eyes and turned back to the other woman. "Thanks for that."

The woman smiled. "No worries. Is your friend okay?"

"I literally just met her. I think she may be a little intoxicated so I'm trying to help her out. Both our flights have been cancelled." Addie explained.

"Yeah same here. Cassiopeia Zephyr. Cassie for short."

"Addie. Nice to meet you."

"Uh, what is your friend doing?" Cassie asked, pointing to where Selene had ignored the crowd lining up and positioned herself at the desk.

"Oh, this isn't going to go down well." Addie sighed, and feeling responsible for her new acquaintance, hurried after her, apologizing to the people she had passed in the queue. Cassie followed her.

"…what do you mean I can't speak to a manager? That's preposterous! I'm here to get on a damned airplane and that's what I intend to do, so go and…" Selene stopped as Addie gently grabbed her arm.

"You can't just jump the line, Selene. We have to wait our turn," Addie explained, trying to pull her back, but Selene wouldn't have a bar of it as she turned her attention back to the mortified-looking airline staff.

"Surely there must be someone I can speak to. I need to get on a plane. I don't even care which one!" She turned back, and leaning forward, with both of her palms pressed against the counter, Selene looked into the eyes of the ground crew. "You will find a plane for my friends and me. Now."

To everyone's surprise, the staff member nodded, "Yes. Of course." And walked away. Satisfied, Selene walked over to the empty rows of seats and sat down, her hands folded carefully in her lap. Addie hesitantly sat beside her, while Cassie remained standing.

"How did you do that?" Cassie asked.

"Do what?" Selene asked, a frown darkening her features.

"It was like you did some kind of mind control over him or something," Cassie explained.

Selene rolled her eyes. "I did no such thing. He was just clearly smart enough to see that I wasn't going to take no for an answer."

Cassie raised her eyebrows but said nothing further as she continued her casual pace up in front of them.

Addie leaned back in her chair and closed her eyes, suddenly feeling sapped of her energy, as though all the people in the room where draining it from her. Her eyes flew open as a rather loud male voice boomed before them.

"Ladies, I overheard the discussion you had with the staff a moment ago..." he started.

"I'm pretty sure the whole terminal heard the conversation," Cassie said dryly, and Addie couldn't help but grin at her. Selene ignored them both as she inspected the man, one eyebrow raised as she looked over his smart, casual attire that was complete with discrete high-end fashion logos.

"You were saying?" Selene prompted.

"Yes, where are my manners. I'm Duke Dillinger. Sir Duke Dillinger." He held his hand out and Selene accepted the grasp, but rather than shake it, he leaned over and placed a kiss on the top of her hand as though addressing royalty.

"Sir Duke?" Cassie asked, unsuccessfully stifling a giggle, and Addie had to hide her own smirk behind a feigned yawn. Both Duke and Selene ignored them.

"Where were you ladies flying to?" Duke asked.

"New York," Addie replied.

"I had just planned to get on the first plane that had a spare seat," Cassie added with a shrug.

"Monaco," Selene replied serenely.

"Monaco?" Cassie mouthed to Addie.

"Well, I don't know if I can be of much help, but if you're wanting to get out of here, I have a private jet prepping that you're more than welcome to join me on. We're flying to New Orleans via JFK."

"But I thought all the planes were grounded?" Addie asked.

"All commercial flights, yes. But there are ways to get around it when you fly privately," Duke said with a smug air. "You may have better luck getting a flight to Monaco out of JFK?"

Selene nodded. "I think that sounds like a much better plan than sitting around here." She rose to her feet.

"Wait, are you just going to go off with him? You don't even know him!" Addie said as she also rose to her feet.

"Do you want to hang around a crowded airport indefinitely or get out of here?" she asked matter-of-factly.

Addie looked to Cassie who shrugged, "Yeah, I guess I want to get out of here too."

"Good. Duke, thank you for generous offer. I would be more than happy to pay for our seats." Selene stated.

Duke held up his hands, "Not necessary. It will just be nice to have some company to be honest. But I didn't get your name?"

"Oh, how rude of me!" Selene exclaimed. "I'm Selene Beaufort, and this is Addie Naya, and, uh…"

"I'm Cassie Zephyr," Cassie said, extending her hand.

"Wonderful. Let me escort you to my private jet." Duke said, leading the way.

"I have a feeling this is going to be awesome," Cassie grinned at them. Addie smiled back as she followed, but she couldn't help but feel like something was about to happen.

***

Addie watched the clouds below, only absently aware of the conversation of the others around her. In her eagerness to escape her life, she had conveniently forgotten how little she actually enjoyed flying. In fact, she downright hated it. Thanks to the storm thundering below them, the flight was bumpy to say the least, and Addie had spent the whole flight gripping the armrests of the comfortable leather chair.

"Are you okay?" Cassie asked as she sat in the chair opposite, looking incredibly relaxed in comparison.

"Yep. Fine," Addie lied, knowing she wasn't fooling anyone. She looked up as a phone next to the door to the cockpit rang and the steward promptly answered. Without a word, she listened briefly before hanging up the phone and walking over to Duke. Apologizing for interrupting his conversation with Selene, she leaned over and whispered in his ear before gathering up glasses and empty plates.

"What's going on?" Addie asked, her voice coming out a little high-pitched as she struggled to contain her nerves.

"It seems we're having some engine trouble and need to make an emergency landing," Duke announced calmly, swinging his chair around to face the front of the cabin and putting on his seatbelt.

Addie looked down at her hands, torn between wanting to fasten her seatbelt and not wanting to let go of the chair.

"Here, let me." Cassie got up and fastened the seatbelt for her, before sitting back in her seat and fastening her own.

"Thank you," Addie replied as the plane hit an air pocket and dropped dramatically. She squeezed her eyes shut as her stomach lurched like she was on the rollercoaster from hell. They fell through the clouds and Addie tried to ignore the high-pitched squeal coming from the engine. The plane shook violently as her breaths came in rapid gasps while she silently prayed for a safe landing. As the plane bucked up and down, she felt the leather of the seat split under her right hand from the pressure of her fingernail against it. Her heart pounded so fiercely that her chest hurt and as she prepared herself for imminent impact, Addie regretted that she had spent the past years of her life abiding by her husband's expectations instead of carving out her own path.

Chapter Three

Cassie

With both her hands cupped against the window, Cassie peered out into the night, trying to see where they were. She had never seen such a pervasive darkness—in fact she didn't think she had ever been any place where there wasn't 24/7 lighting. Cassie wasn't exactly the outdoorsy type. It worried her a little that she wasn't as relieved at their landing as she should be. Her last thoughts as the plane heaved was that she was finally going to see her family again. Now all she felt was a deep sadness welling within her as though they had been taken from her a second time. Quickly wiping the tears from her eyes, she looked across to Addie, who was still gripping the arm rests of her chair for dear life, her eyes squeezed shut. Cassie reached over and tapped her on the knee.

"Addie? We've landed. You can open your eyes now."

"If you could call that a landing," Selene said scathingly, a napkin pressed to forehead.

"Are you okay?" Cassie asked.

"I'm fine. I just hit my head against the window frame and cut the side of my forehead. I'll live," Selene replied. Cassie wasn't certain, but thought the woman almost looked gleeful about her injury, as though it was some kind of battle wound.

"All in all, I rather think the pilot did a fabulous job, all things considered. Could have been much worse," Duke said, unfastening his seatbelt and rising from his chair. "If you ladies will excuse me, I'm just going to have a chat with the pilot and see when we're likely to be off again."

Cassie got up from her seat and stretched. Addie still had her eyes closed, but from her loosened grip on the arm rests it appeared that she was relaxing somewhat.

"Can you see anything out your side of the plane?" she asked Selene.

Selene tried to look out of her window. "Not really. It's just dark. We must be in the middle of nowhere."

Cassie looked up as Duke reappeared from the cockpit, followed by the pilot.

"Looks like we're in a spot of trouble, I'm afraid. We'll have to stay here for the night, at the very least, while the pilot tries to fix whatever the problem with the plane is. Apparently, there is a small town just up the road where you should have no problem finding lodgings for this evening…"

"Hold on a second. Firstly, where the hell are we, and secondly, why can't we just stay here for the duration?" Cassie demanded.

Duke cleared his throat, and with a slight frown to his otherwise-cheerful features he continued, "We're in a little town called Auberon, or so I'm told. The pilot tells me that due to the engine damage it's not safe to reside within the fuselage until they know exactly what the problem is. They can't risk an explosion." Duke chuckled and Cassie frowned, wondering how it was in any way amusing.

"It's fine," Addie stated, now recovered, "I'll just book an Uber and we'll go find somewhere to stay. I'm keen to get off this plane anyway."

Cassie sighed, her hands on her hips as she watched Addie fish her phone from her handbag. Addie held the phone up in the air, waving it around as she tried to get reception.

"Let me try." Cassie stated, walking over to where her own handbag sat nestled under her chair. To her dismay she had no reception either.

"What about you Selene?" Cassie turned to find Selene already trying to get reception on her own phone before she shook her head.

"What about the cockpit radio? Can the pilot arrange someone from the town to come and pick us up?" Cassie asked Duke.

"I'm afraid not. The pilot said the communications system was damaged during landing and he has no idea how long it will take before it's up and running again. I think it's for the best if you go into town and I will send word once we have an ETA on our departure."

"Wait, you're not coming with us?" Selene exclaimed in alarm.

"I'm sorry my dear, but I have too much money invested in this craft to leave it unsupervised. The pilot assures me it's only a short walk up the road to the town…"

"Walk? You want us to walk? In the middle of the night? In a strange place?" Selene's voice increased in volume with each statement.

"Come on ladies, let's just get out of here," Cassie suggested, scowling at Duke as she threw her handbag over her shoulder. "I don't imagine it would be too much trouble to have our bags?"

"We don't have to carry our own bags into town too, do we?" Selene groaned.

"It's probably best," Duke nodded enthusiastically, "You know, just in case of fire…or worse."

"We all wanted an adventure, so here we have it. Let's go!" Cassie announced, and made her way over to where one of the stewards unlocked the door.

"I never said I wanted an adventure. I wanted a holiday in Monaco, surrounded by luxury and handsome men…" Selene replied with a sigh as she reluctantly got up from the comfortable chair.

The three women stepped out of the plane onto what felt like thick, lush, grass.

"Bloody hell!" Cassie exclaimed as she looked around. They were in an open field bordered by tall trees. Reaching back into her handbag, she pulled out her phone and turned on the torchlight, Selene and Addie following suit. They stood by as Duke and the pilot retrieved their bags.

"If you head off in that direction, you will find the road into town on the other side of the trees. I saw it as we were landing. It's really not far." The pilot reassured them.

"Yeah, thanks," Cassie said and rolled her eyes, knowing he wouldn't be able to see her. Using the light from their torches they dragged their suitcases along the grass, pausing every few meters to allow Selene to catch up.

"Why don't you just take those high heels off?" Addie asked. "It would make it much easier for you to walk."

"I am not walking barefoot like some…some…hippie!" Selene huffed.

Cassie chuckled to herself. She wasn't sure what it was, but she found herself enjoying the company of these two women. Despite the fact they didn't seem to have anything in common, Cassie felt drawn to them and admitted to herself that she hadn't felt this relaxed around anyone since she had lost her family. Pausing once again to wait for Selene, Cassie lifted her head and looked at the dark, overcast sky and thought to herself how nice it would be to have some moonlight to guide their way. As she watched, the clouds slowly parted, revealing a full moon. Cassie's mouth fell open as she stared, wondering if she had somehow made it happen.

Don't be ridiculous, of course you didn't. It was just a coincidence.

"Oh wow, check out the moon! How beautiful!" Addie exclaimed, walking past Cassie as Selene caught up again.

As they reached the tree line, Cassie turned back towards the plane and saw Duke still standing in the doorway, illuminated by the light of the cabin. He lifted a hand in farewell, and it was all Cassie could do not to give him the finger in response. Reminding herself that they still needed him to get out of there, she simply nodded and followed her new friends into the woods.

Chapter Four

Selene

Selene almost danced with relief as they finally broke free of the trees and found themselves on the side of the road.

"So, town should be just up the road, right?" she asked with a newfound enthusiasm.

"Apparently," Cassie replied with a smile. Even Addie seemed to be in better spirits now they were on the last leg of a long day.

"Great. I'm dying to take these shoes off," Selene said. Cassie and Addie turned and looked at her before all three of them burst out laughing.

As they walked, and walked, their spirits slowly dwindled as the road stretched on before them with no sign of any town.

"Are we going the right way?" Addie asked.

"This was the direction the pilot told us to go," Cassie replied, pulling her suitcase towards her as she stopped walking. "Should we keep going this way? Or should we turn back and try the other direction?"

"Honestly, I have no idea," Addie sighed.

"This has got to be the most ridiculous day on record," Selene huffed as she took one stiletto off, then the other; as Cassie and Addie watched on, she raised them over her head and threw them into the trees. Cassie and Addie laughed and cheered.

"You have some spunk after all, Selene. I like it!" Cassie grinned at her.

"That was actually kind of liberating," Selene admitted. "Let's just keep going this way. We have to find signs of life at some stage, right?"

"I sure hope so," Cassie replied with a sigh and started walking again.

They had only gone another few meters when bright lights approached from behind. They all turned, shielding their eyes against the sudden brightness.

"It's a car!" Cassie cried and started waving her arms in front of her, hoping the driver would stop. They were in luck.

A huge Jeep-looking vehicle pulled up alongside them, and the window wound down to reveal a handsome, albeit scruffy-looking young man.

"Evening ladies. What's got the three of you walking along here at night?" he asked.

Cassie gave him a quick rundown of their misfortunes and Selene took the opportunity to observe the stranger. She found him exceedingly handsome in a rugged, country-type of way, completely opposite to her straight-laced and prim husband. This man had sandy blonde hair that partially fell across his forehead, with striking cheekbones and a strong jaw. He was wearing a long-sleeved flannel shirt which was folded halfway up his forearm, which was leaning on the open window. Even with a shirt on, Selene could tell his arms were muscular. Very muscular. Again, nothing like her husband. He turned and looked at her, and she felt an instant flutter in her stomach as their eyes met. A smile tugged at the side of his mouth and Selene absently chewed on her lower lip.

"Selene?" Cassie nudged her and she jumped, mortified as she realized they were waiting for her to answer, yet she had no idea what the question was.

"Uh, sorry, I wasn't listening." She said haughtily, as though she had better things to do. Expecting him to cower as she raised her eyebrow at him, she was taken aback as he chuckled. His laugh was deep and throaty, and she felt a rush of heat to her cheeks at the sound. Selene was grateful for the dark.

"Marek just asked if we would like a lift," Cassie explained patiently.

"Marek?" Selene replied.

"At your service," the man said, giving her a little wave. "You ladies are still miles from town. I'm more than happy to give you a ride if you like."

"Yes, please. That would be amazing," Selene declared. Leaving her bags where they were she approached the car. Marek climbed out of the driver's seat.

"Here, you can sit in the front with me," Marek instructed eagerly as he hurried around to the other side of the car and opened the door for her.

"Thank you," she said quietly as she climbed in awkwardly, not used to having to climb up into a car. Selene frowned as she caught Marek trying to hide a smirk, and she grabbed the door from him and pulled it shut. His smirk turned into a grin. "I'll just get your bags, shall I?" he said, walking back around the front of the car.

"That would be lovely, thank you!" Selene replied loudly, folding her arms across her chest.

Addie and Cassie loaded the rest of the bags into the rear of the car before climbing into the back seat. Marek got into the driver's seat, flicking a quick sideways glance at Selene as he gently pressed his foot to the pedal. Selene pretended that she hadn't noticed, looking out of her window instead.

"Oh my god, it feels so good to be sitting down again. My back is killing me!" exclaimed Addie.

"I'm not surprised." Marek said. "Dragging all those bags through those woods is no mean feat."

"You can say that again," Addie replied with a yawn.

Less than ten minutes later, Selene edged forward in her seat as they saw a sign illuminated by the warm yellow glow of a streetlamp that read Auberon Township. The loose dirt road gave way to concrete as they crossed a narrow bridge, before turning to cobblestone on the other side.

"Welcome to Auberon," Marek said, turning to flash Selene a smile. She could only stare back in response as his smile sent a pleasant shiver through her. Hearing Addie and Cassie's appreciative exclamations from the backseat, Selene forced her gaze from Marek and looked out the window. Her mouth fell open as she took in their new town, grateful that Marek had slowed down. The town was well lit; the streets were lined with quaint wrought-iron lamps that flooded the streets with warm, yellow light. Selene thought it looked so much more welcoming than the cold fluorescent lights that lined the streets back home. The buildings that lined either side of the road were all double story and built either close together or adjoining; they were reminiscent of a medieval village that had been preserved in time. Despite her love of all things modern and fashionable, Selene found herself drawn to Auberon.

"Here we are," Marek announced, as he pulled up along the curb in front of a large building on the corner. The sounds of music, laughter and multiple conversations spilled out onto the street and Selene found herself equal parts repulsed and intrigued.

"Well come on then, you're not going to stay in the car all night, are you?" Cassie joked from the sidewalk. Selene reached for the door handle, but before she could open the door, Marek was on the other side, opening it for her. She swung around, about to get out when she froze.

"What is it?" Marek asked.

"I, uh, threw my shoes into the forest," Selene admitted, glaring at Addie and Cassie who burst out laughing as though it was the funniest thing they had ever heard.

"Well that's okay, I'm sure no one will notice. You can get a room sorted and go straight up if you want to. If it turns out you've packed a spare pair of shoes, then you can head back downstairs for dinner and a few drinks. I bet you ladies must be starving," Marek said.

"I've been fantasizing about food for hours," Addie admitted, somehow setting herself and Cassie off into another fit of giggles. Much to Selene's relief, Marek seemed oblivious to their hilarity.

"Would you like me to carry your bags inside for you before I head off?" he offered.

"You're not staying?" Selene blurted out before she knew what she was saying.

"We're fine; thank you so much, Marek," Cassie stated as she reached over and grabbed Selene's hand. "You've saved us enough for one evening."

Marek smiled and gave them a nod before helping Addie and Cassie to unload their bags as Selene watched on, distracted by Marek's height. She thought he looked like a clean and less-hairy version of a Viking.

"Well, enjoy your evening, ladies. It was nice to meet you," Marek said, though he looked straight at Selene. She gave him a little wave as he climbed back into the car and drove off.

"If you think I'm carrying your bags inside for you, you have another thing coming," Cassie warned, half-joking. Selene looked over her shoulder at Marek's car in the distance, before gathering her bags and following Addie and Cassie inside, her bare feet all but forgotten.

She stood against the wall as Cassie boldly approached the bar to enquire about a room. Selene felt overwhelmed as she took in their surroundings. She had never been in a tavern before. The noise was overwhelming, and she found herself both enthralled and appalled at their boisterous behavior of the patrons. Though Marek had been right—no one paid the slightest bit of attention to her bare feet.

"Isn't this exciting?" Addie exclaimed as she grabbed Selene's arm enthusiastically. Selene couldn't think of anything to say and was grateful when Cassie reappeared before them.

"Okay, so do you want the good news or the bad news?" she yelled in order to be heard over the noise.

"The good of course!" Addie yelled back.

"So they have some rooms free," Cassie confirmed.

"What's the bad news then?" Selene had to ask three times before Cassie heard her.

"Oh! The bad news is there are only two rooms. A double bed in one room and two singles in the other," Cassie advised.

"Well I don't care where I sleep, I'll just be grateful to crawl into bed," Addie admitted.

"Same here," Cassie agreed.

"Well, that's settled then" Selene said, relieved.

"It is?" Addie asked.

"Yes. You two don't mind where you sleep, so it makes sense you two take the single beds and I take the double," Selene confirmed, taking the key from Cassie's hand and dragging her bags towards the stairs. She was eager to get away from the noise. She didn't see the bemused expression Addie and Cassie shot at each other.

None of them noticed the hooded figure watching them from the shadows.

Chapter Five

Addie

Rolling over, Addie stretched, her muscles protesting after the adventure of the previous day. Yet she found herself smiling. Their little misadventure was just what the doctor ordered. She sat up to find Cassie already showered and dressed and sitting on the end of her bed while she tied up the laces of her shoes.

"Good morning." Addie said, sitting up on her elbows.

"Hey!" Cassie turned and smiled. "How did you sleep?"

"Like a baby. In fact, I can't remember the last time I slept that well." Addie replied.

"Right!" announced Cassie, arising from the bed with a spritely jump. "I'm going to wake Selene if she's not up already and then go and see about some breakfast and an update on the plane."

Cassie closed the door behind her. Addie reluctantly got out of bed and pulled some clean clothes from the suitcase which lay open on the floor at the foot of her bed. Standing up, Addie swayed as a wave of dizziness washed over her and she saw the room change before her. Gone were the wooden walls and floors, and the humble beds. Instead she stood among lush, green, grass, speckled with tiny flowers. Before her, old stone ruins rose up through the overgrown trees and foliage. In the center of what might have once been a room stood a large stone urn. Addie walked towards it and looked in. There was a tiny blue flickering, like a small flame trying to ignite. Reaching out her hand, she tried to touch it but then the vision vanished. Addie looked around the room, her heart pounding.

What the hell is happening to me?

Addie hurried from the room and headed to the bathroom.

Taking the stairs two at a time, she could hear Selene's outraged complaining before she saw Selene and Cassie with an apologetic-looking innkeeper. Cassie was pacing with her hands on her hips, while Selene stood rigid, her arms folded tightly across her chest.

"Do I want to know?" Addie asked as she approached.

The women all turned around. "The plane's gone!" Selene screeched, throwing her hands up in the air.

"What do you mean, gone?" Addie asked, frowning.

"They left without us." Cassie confirmed. "The message is that apparently it wasn't safe to carry passengers and they will return in a day or two."

"Seriously?" Addie exclaimed, wanting to sound outraged, but in truth she felt relieved. Something about Auberon was calling to her and she wanted an opportunity to at least explore a little before they left.

"Can we use your phone?" Cassie asked, turning back to the innkeeper.

"I'm sorry, it's still out from last night's storm."

"Of course, it is." Cassie replied with a sigh.

"So, what does that mean? We're stuck here indefinitely? I don't want to stay here another night!" Selene exclaimed.

Before anyone could respond, a car horn sounded from outside; the three women went to the door and found Marek's Jeep parked out the front, with him leaning casually against it. Addie smiled, noting he had made some effort with his appearance since last night and though he greeted all three of them, it was clear he was already holding a flame for Selene.

"I heard about the plane leaving and thought I would swing by and see if you needed anything." Marek stated.

"Actually, do you know if there is other accommodation if we have to stay here another couple of nights?" Selene asked, stepping forward onto the pavement.

"You mean the tavern's not to your liking?" Marek asked, smiling; Addie was amazed to see Selene blush.

"I mean…it's not…I just…" she stammered, looking from Addie to Cassie for help but they both just grinned at her.

"I'm just teasing, Selene," Marek said as he stepped away from the car. "Though I think there may actually be a place you could rent for a night or two. It wouldn't be cheap though."

"Oh, that's not a problem. We'll take it," Selene said.

"Uh, do you want to see it first?" Addie asked.

Selene shrugged, "If it's expensive it's bound to be nice, right?"

Addie looked from Selene to Cassie, who shrugged, "There's some logic in that."

"Okay then," Addie confirmed. "Let's go and have a look."

"Wait," Selene held out her hands, "Let's go and get our things first. You know, so if we like it, we don't have to waste time coming back."

Cassie shook her head. "You heard what she said."

Within minutes the women were back in Marek's car and he was driving them through the winding streets. The town was even more beautiful in the daytime; Addie found herself getting lost in the scenery as the road wound around up the hill. She was pulled from her daydreaming by Selene's exclamations.

"Oh my! Will you look at that! It's stunning!"

Addie leaned over to look out of Cassie's window and saw a magnificent house rising up the side of the mountain. It was four stories high, but the bottom two stories were built into the side of the mountain, so that only the top two stories were visible from the street view.

"Welcome to Auberon Manor," Marek announced as he pulled the car around to the front of the house. "I trust this is more to your liking?" He glanced over at Selene who could only nod in reply as she opened the door and got out for a better look.

"Is anyone else living here?" Addie asked as she and Cassie also got out of the car.

"Nope. It's actually been empty for ages." He walked around the back of the car and started lifting their bags out. "I have to head off to work now, but I know the landlord so will ask him to drop around at some point today to go over the finer details and answer any questions you might have."

"That would be great, thanks," Addie replied, accepting the keys from him.

They waived him off and as Addie approached the enormous carved wooden door, she felt a surge of excitement, as though she was about to unlock endless possibilities, not just a front door.

It creaked as she pushed it open, and they gasped in unison at the two-story foyer complete with vaulted ceiling.

"Oh, my…" whispered Selene.

"Yeah, I second that," Cassie agreed as they gazed at the immaculate art deco interior.

"Marek said this place has been empty for ages, but you wouldn't know it. Everything looks like it's in perfect condition," Addie commented as she walked around the foyer.

"Someone clearly loves the place," Cassie agreed. "I get first pick of the bedrooms!" she yelled and dashed up the stairs.

"Wait! I want to pick one too!" Selene cried as she ascended the stairs as quickly as she could without actually breaking into a run.

Addie watched them go—there was somewhere else she wanted to check out first. Walking through to the right wing of the house, she finally found the largest kitchen she had ever seen, and she clasped her hands to her chest with glee.

This is it. I've died and gone to heaven.

Addie started opening and closing cupboards as well as the double-doored fridge, but the kitchen was completely devoid of any food. Leaving the kitchen, Addie walked back through the foyer and was about to take her bags upstairs when she spotted the old-fashioned phone sitting in a lit alcove in the opposite wall. She strode over, holding her breath as she picked up the receiver and held it to her ear. A dial tone buzzed in her ear and Addie excitedly called out to Cassie and Selene as she dialed the airport. If they couldn't tell them when Duke would be back with his plane—assuming he was coming back—then they should be able to tell where and when the next-closest flight would be.

By the time Selene and Cassie arrived at her side, her excitement had turned to confusion.

"What is it?" Cassie asked.

Addie covered the mouthpiece of the phone with her hand, "They're trying to tell me that no private planes departed from the airport last night."

"Well clearly it did, because here we are." Cassie retorted frowning, her hands once again on her hips.

Addie shrugged, unsure what to tell them, and returned to the phone call, "You see, I was supposed to be on flight J689 to New York, but it was cancelled…what?" Addie's eyes widened as she stared at her friends in disbelief.

"What is it?" Cassie hissed.

Addie covered the phone again, "They said my flight was never cancelled; it departed as planned."

"But we saw the board! It said cancelled!" Cassie exclaimed.

"Ask about my flight, J323 to Monaco," Selene instructed.

The response was the same.

"Well can you tell me when the next return flight is?" Addie closed her eyes and pinched the bridge of her nose. She could hardly believe what she was hearing. Hanging up the phone, she turned to Cassie and Selene.

"So? Are we leaving?" Selene asked.

"It doesn't look like it," Addie replied slowly.

"What do you mean?" Cassie asked.

"According to the woman I just spoke to, our flights departed as scheduled, and they have no record of any private jets taking off." She confirmed.

"Well, it's a private jet," Selene stated. "Don't they just come and go as they please?"

Cassie shook her head, "No. Every flight needs clearance for take-off and landing, or else they would have collisions all over the place."

"Okay then, so you're right. This doesn't make any sense." Selene conceded.

"What's more, they said the nearest airport is a day's drive away, but there aren't any flights home for the week," Addie continued to explain.

"How does that make any sense?" Cassie exclaimed.

"It doesn't," Addie said with a sigh.

"So what are we going to do?" Selene asked.

Addie looked at her new friends and shrugged, "Honestly, I don't know. This is going to sound crazy, but I kind of feel like we're supposed to be here; that we were supposed to meet at the airport and come here together."

"You're right, that does sound crazy," Selene said dryly.

"No, I think you're right Addie," Cassie agreed. "It's been mayhem, but I've felt more alive in the past 18 hours than I have in a very long time."

"When you put it like that, I would have to agree," conceded Selene.

"So what does it mean? It still doesn't answer the question as to what we should do next," Addie quizzed.

"I know but…what the…?" Cassie trailed off as she stared past Addie towards the large windows overlooking a small courtyard.

"What is it?" Selene asked, leaning forward.

"Look!" Cassie said, pointing towards the trees that bordered the rear of the courtyard. Selene gasped, covering her mouth with her hand dramatically as they saw the tall, hooded figure standing among the trees.

"Do you think that's the landlord?" Selene whispered.

"No, Selene. I'm pretty sure that's not the landlord," Addie hissed.

The three of them stood there, waiting for the figure to move, but when nothing happened, Cassie stormed forward, yanking open the glass sliding door.

"Cassie, stop! It could be dangerous!" Addie yelled after her, but Cassie was on a rampage.

"Hey you! What the hell do you think you're doing lurking in the trees like some kind of pervert? Show yourself you coward or else piss off!" The figure slowly turned around until its back was facing Cassie. She stopped, waiting for it to keep walking, but it stood perfectly still. Cassie looked over her shoulder to where Selene and Addie were now at the door; she shrugged.

"Why don't you just come back inside, Cassie, and we can call the police?" Selene asked.

The figure took slow steps into the forest and Cassie started following.

"Cassie! What are you doing? Are you nuts?" Addie called out.

"Maybe!" Cassie called back.

"God damn it! We have to go after her!" Addie exclaimed, stepping out into the courtyard.

"Uh, pretty sure we don't. You realize she's literally following a stranger into a forest, right?" Selene stated.

"Come on!" Addie grabbed Selene by the arm and dragged her along, just as they lost sight of Cassie through the trees. As they caught up, Addie realized they were actually walking along a narrow path that weaved its way through the trees.

"What are you thinking?" Addie hissed.

Cassie shrugged. "I just felt like we were supposed to follow him. So I did."

Addie opened her mouth to argue, but quickly closed it again. She had to admit, she was equally as intrigued.

The path continued as they came out on the other side of the trees, before reaching the cliff edge. As they stood in awe of the majestic view, the hooded figure continued walking towards a narrow stone bridge that was mostly engulfed by vines and moss.

"Come on!" whispered Cassie, and they hurried after him.

"Oh my god, that is so far down! I can't!" Selene screeched halfway along the bridge after making the mistake of looking down.

"Here, take my hand. I'll help you across," Addie offered, not wanting to admit that, while the view was spectacular, she was as terrified as Selene. It was a sheer drop on either side of the bridge, and they were so high up that Addie couldn't even see what awaited them should they fall. Cassie, on the other hand, seemed completely oblivious as she neared the other side a few feet behind the hooded figure.

Focusing on placing one foot in front of the other, Addie led Selene across, her gratitude at reaching the other side short lived as she found herself surrounded by ancient ruins. Like the bridge, the ruins were also overrun with foliage, but Addie thought it added to the beauty of the area.

"What is that?" Selene whispered, nudging and pointing to a large stone urn before them.

"I have no idea…" Addie replied, suddenly finding herself mesmerized by the plumes of scented smoke billowing upwards from it. As she watched on, the hooded figure walked around to the other side of the urn to face them. Holding its arms out, it gestured for the women to come closer. Cassie looked at the others and shrugged, "Well, we've come this far."

While Addie didn't quite share her enthusiasm, she stepped up to the urn, dragging Selene alongside her.

"Um, excuse me, but who are you?" Selene asked the figure, but it kept its head down and remained silent.

"Is it just me or is this getting a little awkward?" Addie asked.

Before either woman could answer her, she looked down at the mossy ground beneath her feet. "Can you feel that?" she asked.

"Yeah, I can. It's like there's a vibration coming up through the ground into my feet." Cassie replied.

"It feels weird. I don't like it," Selene said as she shifted her weight from one foot to the other and back again.

As the vibration intensified, it became harder for the women to move—first their feet, and then their bodies.

"Yeah this was a fantastic idea, Cassie! Now we're going to get eaten by Hannibal the Cannibal over there!" hissed Addie as she struggled to raise her hands from her sides.

"Stop being so melodramatic," Cassie hissed back. "I'm almost certain it's not a cannibal."

"Almost certain?" Selene screeched.

Silence...

The women all looked at the hooded figure in surprise, unsure if the voice had come from it or not as it seemed to float all around them. Before them, the smoke in the urn danced higher and higher in a hypnotic dance, ensuring it had their undivided attention. Then, it split into three undulating plumes, each one weaving its way towards the women. Addie squeezed her eyes shut and tried to hold her breath as the smoke neared, but it was no use. Her nose stung and her eyes watered as the smoke forced its way inside her.

All her thoughts fell away, replaced by images that she didn't recognize yet which were familiar somehow. The sound of voices echoed in her ears: generations of women, all talking softly as though beckoning her forward. Addie felt her heartbeat quicken; she was engulfed by a brilliant flash of light before all three of them collapsed to the ground.

As Addie, Cassie and Selene lay unconscious amongst the moss, the plumes of smoke withdrew from their bodies and back into the urn, dwindling into nothingness. The hooded figure raised its hood and the cloak fell to the ground in a heap. There was no one there.

Destiny Unlocked

Chapter One

Addie

Opening her eyes, Addie found herself staring up at the night sky. It was overcast but the brightness of the moon provided some illumination from behind the clouds—enough to see, at least. She frowned, raising herself up onto her elbows to look around. Startled to see Cassie and Selene on the ground on either side of her, Addie pushed herself up onto her knees and crawled over to Cassie's side.

"Cassie! Wake up! Can you hear me?" Addie shouted, shaking her by the shoulder, but she wouldn't waken. Addie crawled over to Selene, but she was the same. Addie sighed with relief to find they were both breathing, but they appeared to be in a deep sleep. She sat back on the grass between them, and massaged her temples with her fingers, willing the headache and the queasiness away. She stared at the stone urn before them, and recalled a fire burning in it, and smoke drifting towards them. Yet it felt like a strange dream, nothing more.

An odd-looking shape caught her attention from where it lay on the ground, slightly obscured by the urn. Forcing herself to her feet, she staggered towards it, recognizing it as a cloak. The dreamlike quality of her memory cleared a little, and she recalled the strange, cloaked figure they'd followed from the manor. Addie leaned over to pick it up, but the minute her fingers touched the course fabric her mind flooded with a barrage of images.

I can see the figure, but it's not wearing the cloak. It's so tall, inhumanly so, and its grey hair is long and dirty, matted with leaves and twigs. I can't make out if the creature is male or female—or even human at all. It's raising its head like it knows I can see it… I don't want it to see me.

The cloak grew hot against her fingertips and Addie let it drop to the ground, as though it was on fire.

What the hell was that? Where did the figure disappear to?

Feeling a little dizzy from the suddenness of the vision, Addie reached out to steady herself against the urn. It felt slightly warm, as though it still held the caress of the day's sunlight, and as Addie felt better, she peered into it. Addie thought she could see something lying in the bottom, and with her curiosity getting the better of her, she reached into the urn as far as she could. Her fingertips brushed against something cool and smooth, and a sudden rush of air blew past her, causing her hair to fly up into the air. She tried to withdraw her arm from the urn, but there was a force pulling her downwards. Her heart pounded as the bottom of the urn seemed to disappear, and in its place the purple smoke returned, swirling and vibrant.

This can't be happening. This isn't real. Wake up, Addie. Wake up!

Addie fought against the pull, but it was of no use and as she felt her feet lift off the ground, she screamed out to Cassie and Selene, yet she could hardly hear her own voice over the roar of the swirling portal of smoke. There was nothing left to do but close her eyes.

Chapter Two

Cassie

Groaning, Cassie sat up; her hand pressed to her forehead. "What happened? I feel like I've got a killer hangover."

"What's going on?" Cassie turned around to see Selene sitting up, looking as confused as Cassie felt.

"I had a weird dream about purple smoke…" Cassie murmured.

"I was just thinking the same thing…" Selene agreed.

"Wait, where's Addie?" Cassie asked, frantically looking around as she rose to her feet. "Addie!" She walked over to Selene and helped her to her feet. They both walked around the small grove, calling for their friend as they looked for any sign of her.

"Where could she have gone?" Selene asked.

"I have no idea." Cassie replied, peering into the urn. She couldn't see anything, so she reached in, feeling along the bottom, but there was only cold stone.

"Why are you looking for Addie in the urn?" Selene asked.

"Obviously, I'm not. I just, I don't know, had a weird feeling." Cassie replied, giving the inside of the urn a last pat down.

"I don't like this. I don't remember what happened, or how we got here." Selene said, wrapping her arms around herself.

"Well, that's what we need to find out." Cassie stated as she stood up, clutching at her stomach as a wave of nausea swept over her. "Ugh, I feel awful."

"Join the club." Selene added, pinching the bridge of her nose with her thumb and forefinger.

"What did that smoke do to us?" Cassie asked.

"Is that a cloak?" Selene asked, pointing to a pile of material around the other side of the urn, but making no move to look closer.

Cassie rolled her eyes and strode towards it, picking it up with both hands and holding it up. Though she held the shoulder of the cloak above her head, the fabric still pooled on the grass at her feet. "Whoever wore this was super tall. It smells like…damp rotting leaves."

"Charming." Selene scoffed.

"Come to think of it, the last thing I remember was someone standing here, wearing this."

"Yeah, I vaguely have that recollection too." Selene confessed.

"The figure…" Cassie said, looking around as her memories trickled back. "There was someone lurking around the manor, remember?"

"The figure we saw lurking outside the manor was tall, but not as tall as you're suggesting" Selene stated, folding her arms across her chest.

"I don't know, maybe it was crouching or hid it somehow? I have no idea, that's just what I remember." Cassie answered.

"Great. So we followed a strange figure into the forest, inhaled some weird smoke, and lost Addie. Does that sound about right?" Selene summarized.

Cassie shook her head. "Okay, this is crazy. Whatever that smoke was, it must have been some kind of hallucinogen, or something, and we're just experiencing the effects of a weird-ass trip. Probably just a prank from the locals—you know, show the fancy city folk a thing or two."

"You're right, that is crazy." Selene replied.

Cassie groaned. "Well, what *do* we know? We woke up here after who knows how long, and Addie is missing."

"Do you think maybe she went back to the manor?" Selene asked.

"Maybe. Though I can't see her leaving without us or walking through those woods alone." Cassie replied. "In saying that, I don't think we have any hope of finding her in the dark. We should go back to the manor and call Marek."

"What, back across that bridge?" Selene gasped.

"Well, I don't know of any other way, do you?" Cassie asked, trying to contain her impatience.

"No. It's just pretty much dark now, and that bridge was long and narrow. Aren't you in the least bit concerned?" Selene asked.

Cassie thought about it for a moment. "No. I mean, we came across it easily enough. It's in good condition; if we just take it slowly, we'll be fine."

"Well, I don't share your enthusiasm, but I guess we don't have any choice." Selene said. "Lead the way."

Cassie led them through the ruins, towards the bridge, and as she tried to see the other side through the increasing darkness, she noted that it seemed a lot further than she remembered.

"I wish there was more light so we could see better." Cassie said aloud, looking up at the sky. As soon as she'd uttered the words, the clouds parted, revealing the full moon as it shone its bright light down upon them like a beacon in the night.

"Did you just…?" Selene asked slowly.

"Of course not." Cassie scowled. "It's just a coincidence."

"Either way, I'm grateful for the light, so let's get a move on before the clouds move back over again." Selene demanded, gently nudging Cassie in the back.

"Why am I taking the lead?" Cassie asked.

"Because you're the one that led us over it in the first place, and I'm scared shitless." Selene advised.

Cassie took a deep breath. "We can do this together," she said, looking over her shoulder as she reached out her hand. Selene hesitated for a moment before taking it. With their hands clasped, Cassie gave a quick nod and took the first slow steps over the bridge.

Chapter Three

Addie

Surrounded by darkness, Addie could feel herself falling with no sense of whether she was up or down or even sideways. It reminded her of one of her favorite books, Alice In Wonderland, and she was Alice, falling through the center of the Earth.

Suddenly, her thoughts were overtaken by a vivid scene.

I hear the screeching of tires—a vehicle is travelling too quickly. I'm standing at the entrance to the manor, looking out across the circular driveway. It's night, and the light in the forecourt spills a golden glow over everything. I can hear Selene and Cassie walking through the house and coming up behind me, but I don't turn around. I see Marek's jeep approaching—he's speeding. The jeep slows considerably when he sees us standing there and he pulls the jeep up in front of us. I see Marek leaning out of the window, looking at each one of us, his eyes wide with panic and his breathing heavy.

The vision ended as Addie crashed into something hard, and she moaned, pulling her throbbing knee to her chest as she rolled on the floor. As she lay there, her eyes started adjusting to the darkness and she slowly sat up and looked around. All around her was dark stone, rising as high as she could see. It looked like a cavern and Addie frowned as she scanned the walls, trying to find an opening or a way out. She was startled by a strange dragging sound coming from somewhere to her left. Peering into the darkness, Addie tried to see the source, her heart pounding in her chest. Just as she was about to look away, certain she was imagining things, the figure moved, alerting her to its presence. Addie gasped, recognizing it as the same figure that they'd followed through the woods to the ruins.

The same figure that led them to the ruins!

Addie couldn't be certain, but it appeared to be staring at her. It was hard to tell because the figure was at least eight feet tall.

That's not possible. It wasn't that tall when we followed it.

The creature released a low, guttural sound —part growl, part moan —which sent a chill through Addie. As much as she wanted to turn away, she didn't think she could move if she tried—her increasing fear had frozen her in place.

When she didn't move, the creature seemed to take that as a sign, for it raised its hand, palm up, and as it stretched out its fingers towards her, a spiral of purple smoke drifted upwards, floating towards her as though it had a life of its own. Closing her eyes, and holding her breath, Addie tried to hold out until the smoke reached her, but when she couldn't hold her breath any longer, she gasped for air. Yet, when she opened her eyes, the smoke had gone, as had the creature. Addie scrambled to her feet, a lump of fear rising in her throat as she thought she was being left behind with no escape. Scanning the walls, she tried to find a way out, when she spotted a faint wisp of the smoke at the other side of the cavern.

Maybe this isn't a good idea. Maybe you should just stay put until Cassie and Selene can find you.

Addie shook the thought away, feeling there was no time to lose. Reaching the wall where she'd seen the smoke, she was surprised to find a passageway. She took a deep breath and stepped inside.

Chapter Four

Selene

As she stepped off the bridge and back onto solid land, Selene let out a loud sigh of relief and looked up at the full moon. "Look!"

As they watched, the clouds moved back over the moon, like curtains across the stage at the end of a show.

Cassie shook her head. "Not a word."

"I didn't say anything." Selene piped up. "But…"

"Not. A. Word." Cassie held up her finger in warning and led the way through the trees and back to the manor, calling out Addie's name as they went.

As she passed through the threshold and back into the house, Selene felt a shiver pass through her, despite the relief she felt at being indoors once more.

"How about we split up and look for her?" Cassie suggested.

"I know it would be quicker," said Selene, "but is it such a wonderful idea to split up when there's a creepy cloaked figure out there somewhere?"

"The figure isn't wearing the cloak anymore, remember?" Cassie replied.

Selene rolled her eyes. "You know what I mean."

Cassie sighed, "Yeah, I do. You're right. Let's do a quick sweep of the house and if we still can't find her, I'm calling Marek."

Selene nodded, letting Cassie lead the way. Despite their loud calls, there was no sign of Addie, so the two women made their way back to the kitchen to call Marek.

"I'll call him if you like." Selene offered, trying to sound like she didn't care one way or the other, but the thought of hearing his voice made her heart quicken.

"Sure," Cassie said, taking a seat at the kitchen island.

Selene grabbed the piece of paper with Marek's number on it, from where Addie had stuck it on the fridge. Walking over to the phone, she stared at the round dial and the clunky, antique handset.

"You don't know how to use a rotary phone, do you?" Cassie asked, and Selene could hear the laughter in her voice, despite her thinly veiled attempt to withhold it.

"Shut up." Selene said sulkily, handing the piece of paper to Cassie, before taking a seat herself.

Who still uses landlines anyway?

Selene tried her best to distract herself, annoyed by how much she wanted to hear Marek's voice.

You're being ridiculous. You just met the guy, and he's hardly your type.

Suddenly, Selene's eyes fell upon the very distraction she was looking for—a liquor cabinet. Sliding off the stool, she flicked a glance over her shoulder to where Cassie was still on the phone, and walked over to the cabinet. As she placed her hands on the doors, she prayed it was stocked with a top shelf gin and some dry vermouth.

Selene excitedly withdrew an unopened bottle of gin, inspecting it briefly before placing it on the ground beside her. She ran her fingers over the labels of the remaining bottles—whiskey, vodka, bourbon, scotch, a variety of schnapps, and Angostura bitters. But no vermouth. Selene sighed.

"So, Marek's on his way." Cassie said as she walked over.

"Oh?" Selene said as dismissively as she could, though she kept facing the bottles of alcohol, worried Cassie would see the sudden flush in her cheeks.

"What have you got there?" Cassie picked up the bottle of gin. "Oh! You read my mind!"

"I wanted to make martinis, but there isn't any vermouth," Selene stated, getting to her feet.

"What do you call that in your hands?" Cassie asked.

"Oh, just some bit…" Selene's mouth fell open as she looked down at an unopened bottle of vermouth. She looked up at Cassie, her eyes wide. "I swear this was a bottle of bitters a second ago."

Cassie burst out laughing, but it quickly fell away when Selene's expression didn't change. "Wait, what? You can't be serious."

"I don't know what to tell you. I was disappointed, because we didn't have any, and then the next thing I know, we do," Selene explained. She could tell from Cassie's expression that she didn't believe her.

"We'll have to talk about it later. I told Marek we'd wait for him out front," Cassie said, placing the bottle of gin on the kitchen island. Selene placed the bottle of vermouth beside it and followed her.

As they opened the front door and stepped out onto the portico, they could already hear Marek's ute coming up the hill at speed. Selene felt a flutter of nerves as he came around the bend, before driving around into the circular driveway and pulling up before them. He looked at them, his breathing heavy as though he'd rushed.

"Hey. Glad to see you're still here." He said, getting out of the car, looking directly at Selene.

"Where else would we be? We're kind of stuck here, remember?" Cassie said.

"Oh. It's just Ravi—the landlord—called me, accusing me of pulling his leg. He said he came up to the house to welcome you and go over the details of your stay here, but there was no answer," Marek explained, running a hand through his sweaty, sandy blond hair.

"Ah, well…" Cassie started, looking over at Selene quickly before continuing. "We went for a walk. You know, exploring the grounds and all that. I guess we just lost track of time."

"Then we lost Addie, so we were looking everywhere for her," Selene added. Her voice came out with a bit of a squeak, and she wished the ground would open up and swallow her.

Marek grinned but said nothing and Selene snuck a glance up at him, watching him intently as he rubbed his short-cropped beard like he was trying to think of what to say.

"So we need to find Addie. I know Auberon must seem quaint to the three of you, but it's not safe to wander around after dark on your own. Especially up here."

"Why?" Selene asked, as panic hit her in the chest. "What's up here that we should worry about?"

"Oh, nothing!" he blurted, flashing her a slight smile. "It's just old, and no one's lived here for so long; you don't know what's out there," he said all too quickly. "Where were you when you last saw her?"

"Well, we went for a walk through the woods and found these old ruins…" Cassie started.

"You found the Auberon Urn?" Marek asked, his eyes wide.

"Uh, yeah. It wasn't like it was hard…" Cassie said slowly, flicking a quick look at Selene.

Marek nodded slowly, rubbing at his beard again.

"Why? Were we not supposed to go there?" Selene asked, puzzled by his reaction. "There weren't any no trespassing signs or anything."

"Evidently," he replied, his blue eyes locked on hers as though he was trying to see into her soul.

Selene chewed on her lower lip, not liking how awkward and strange she felt.

Cassie cleared her throat. "So, like I was saying, we were at the, uh, Auberon Urn and we haven't seen Addie since. We thought maybe she'd come back to the house, but when we got back, we couldn't see any sign of her here either."

"Hmm." Marek said, looking past them into the house. "Do you mind if I use the phone? I should call Ravi."

"Uh, sure. I'll show you…"

"It's fine, thank you, I know where it is." Marek said, striding between them and into the house.

Selene waited until he was out of earshot. "Is it just me, or is he acting strangely?"

"Strangely. Did you see his face when we mentioned the Auberon Urn?" Cassie whispered.

Selene nodded. "Maybe it's some kind of sacred relic that you're not supposed to go near or something. Right now I'm more concerned about finding Addie."

"Agreed," Cassie said, grabbing her arm and leading them through the house to the kitchen where Marek was just hanging up the phone.

"Ravi's on his way," he said, walking over to the windows and looking out into the night towards the bordering trees.

"So, uh, what do we do in the meantime? Should I try to find some flashlights and we can start looking through the woods again?" Cassie asked.

"That won't be necessary." Marek stated, turning to look at them over his shoulder. "Your friend's no longer here."

Chapter Five

Addie

The tunnel was narrow, dank and dark, and all Addie could see was the purple smoke drifting along up ahead. The creature's pace quickened the further along they went and she was struggling to keep up.

Suddenly, she tripped over the uneven terrain, and fell heavily forwards. Groaning, she sat back as she rubbed at her aching knees and elbow. Her arm felt sticky; she was sure her elbow was bleeding, but using the wall for support she pulled herself back to her feet.

Oh crap.

The smoke—and the figure—were both gone.

Addie took a quick glance into the blackness behind her, considering turning back, yet she didn't know how she could get out that way. She knew the only way was forward.

Come on, Addie. You wanted adventure? Well, now you've got it. So put on your big girl pants and keep moving.

Taking a deep breath, Addie hobbled onwards, refusing to acknowledge the pain in her knees and elbow as she used the wall to guide her forwards. She had only walked a short distance when the tunnel ended, and she stepped into a magnificent cavern. It rose so high that the only way she could make out the ceiling was because of the numerous crystal stalactites that hung from it.

Where am I?

In the middle of the cavern was an orb, suspended in mid-air like a giant looking glass filled with smoke. The smoke changed colors—purple, to blue, to green, and then grey. Addie felt mesmerized by it, and she walked towards it without a second thought. As she neared, she could have sworn she heard voices. They were quiet at first, and Addie strained to hear them. Yet they quickly grew louder, more urgent. They sounded like they were coming from within the orb, but also all around her. The voices made her feel on edge and even though she couldn't understand the words, the tone was loud and clear.

Danger. Get out. Now.

Addie conceded there was no other choice—she had to go back the way she came. Yet as she ran to the wall behind her, the tunnel was no longer there.

That's impossible!

Thinking she must have become disoriented, she ran her hands along the wall. She ran the entire way around the cavern and there wasn't a single exit. She felt sick to her stomach as panic seized her; the increasing volume did little to calm her.

Suddenly the colored smoke in the orb turned an inky black, and the voices ceased. All but one.

He's here.

Addie pressed her back to the wall, willing herself to disappear into the shadows. The orb trembled with a vibration so strong she could feel it through her feet. As she saw a large, black boot step out from the smoke, she placed a hand over her mouth, fighting against the urge to scream.

A man stepped out, tall and stocky. Dressed all in black, he wore a black cape decorated with gold thread. His long black hair was pulled back and gathered in tiny braids and his beard was long with gold strands woven through it. There was something about his presence that made Addie's skin crawl—her senses were on overdrive as she tried her best to remain out of sight.

"May I suggest, in the future, if you wish to remain out of sight, then perhaps wear something a little more inconspicuous," the man said, slowly turning his head to the side to stare at her. His eyes were the same color gold as the thread.

Addie remained silent, but the man continued as though her response was irrelevant.

"I suppose I should thank you. If it wasn't for your little impromptu arrival, I would still be in the Nethers."

He walked away from the orb, his steps purposeful as Addie slowly slid along the wall in the opposite direction, trying to keep her distance as a thousand questions ran through her head.

Who is this guy?

What is he talking about?

How can I get out of here?

"I have to admit, Adamina, I had my money on Cassiopeia…"

"How do you know my name?" Addie blurted out before she could stop herself.

He paused in his pacing and stared at her, one eyebrow slightly raised. "I can't decide if you're being coy, or if you really don't know…"

Addie kept her expression as neutral as she could as she tried to buy some time.

I've got to get out of here. But how?

Before she could take her next breath, he was in front of her, close enough to reach out and touch her.

How did he move so fast?

Addie gasped and looked from one side to the other, but she knew that she couldn't move in either direction without him reaching her.

I'm trapped.

His gold eyes glinted despite the darkness. "You can't play games with me, Adamina. I know you better than that. Or did you forget?"

"You're a madman! I've never seen you before in my life!" Addie hissed at him, cursing herself for reaching into the urn.

"A madman, yes, I've heard that before," he chuckled to himself, withdrawing a dagger from within the folds of his cape and raising it before him, so the tip rested beneath Addie's chin. "Now tell me how to control the portal, or I will hurt you. You know that I can."

"What portal? What are you talking about?" Addie tried to wriggle away from the knife, but he only poked it harder.

"Do you think I'm a fool? First you use it to trap me in the Nethers for over a hundred years, and then out of nowhere you release me, only to pretend you know nothing of it? If you think I will let you or anyone else send me back there, you have another think coming. Now tell me how it works!" His anger reverberated around the cavern and Addie looked up, fearful that the vibration would send the stalactites falling onto them.

"I told you! I don't know what you're talking about! I don't know who you are or what the Nethers are. I just want to get out of here and get back to my friends!" she spat.

"Friends?" He lowered the knife, chuckling to himself as he rubbed his forehead with his freehand.

"I'm assuming you mean Cassiopeia and Selene? They're here with you?"

"Not *here*, here. But yes."

"Of course they are. And you expected me to believe you have no idea what you're doing. Well, I'm not fooled, and now it's time for you to pay your dues!"

Before he could move, Addie felt like time had frozen, while simultaneously speeding up. Her mouth fell open as she watched both what the man was doing, and what he was *going* to do.

Holy crap!

Addie ducked as time returned to normal, having seen him throw the ball of lightning towards her before he did. Her bruised knees protested as they once again hit the stone, but she knew she didn't have time to waste.

A second ball of lightning exploded into the wall above her, and she covered her head with her hands as she tried to scurry out of the way.

Diving across the cavern floor, she landed heavily on her left shoulder but rolled across the room before his next blow put an actual hole in the wall where she'd just been.

If ever you were going to have actual power to control your destiny, Addie, now is the time to work out what kind of bloody power it is.

Chapter Six

Cassie

W hat do you mean Addie's not here anymore? Of course she's not here. If she was, then we wouldn't have called you." Cassie said, her hands on her hips as she frowned at Marek.

He remained silent, looking out into the night.

Cassie looked to Selene where she stood beside the kitchen island, but she just shrugged her shoulders.

"I told Ravi I'd meet him out the front." Marek said, turning from the window but avoiding looking at either of them as he strode out of the kitchen.

"What the hell was that about?" Cassie asked, sliding onto a stool.

"Maybe he's just worried for Addie, like we are?" Selene suggested.

Cassie shook her head. "No. He knows something. I can feel it."

"Have you always been this suspicious of people?" Selene asked, softening the question with a smile.

"I'm not suspicious, I can just read people and places well. I've always been able to. It's easy enough to see when someone's being shady. People aren't as complex as they like to think they are," Cassie explained, pulling the bottle of vermouth towards her. "Do you think it would be unseemly to have a drink while Addie's missing?"

"Maybe, but I sure could use one," Selene stated as she started rummaging through the cupboards for glasses.

"While we're waiting, how about you try that neat little trick you mentioned earlier? See if it works again?" Cassie suggested, running her fingers over the bottle of vermouth.

"I can tell by the tone in your voice that you don't believe me," Selene said dryly as she placed two glasses on the bench.

"It's more that I'm just the kind of person who needs to see things for myself. Do you think you could do it again?" Cassie asked.

"Do what, exactly?" Selene asked, looking around the kitchen.

"I don't know, maybe you could try turning water into wine." Cassie joked, but as she looked up, she saw the smile on Selene's face as she picked up one of the glasses and filled it with water from the sink. Placing it on the bench between them, Selene stared at it, chewing her lip.

"So?" Cassie asked.

"Hold your horses. I don't know how I did it the first time." Selene snapped.

"Well, you said you were holding the bottle the first time. Maybe you need to hold it?" Cassie suggested, leaning forward on her elbows.

Selene held up her hands and hesitated before closing her eyes. It felt to Cassie like she was taking ages, and it was all she could do not to drum her fingers on the bench top.

Finally, Selene opened her eyes, and Cassie realized she'd been so focused on Selene's motionlessness that she hadn't seen what was happening right in front of her.

"Holy shit! You did it!" Cassie clapped her hands. "Taste it!"

Selene picked up the glass and tentatively held it up to her lips. "Oh, that is so good."

"Let me try." Cassie held her hand out and took a swig, closing her eyes as she savored the mouthful. "I don't know how the hell you did that, but that is the best tasting wine I think I've had in my entire life." When she reopened her eyes, she saw Selene grinning at her.

"What is it?" Cassie asked. "Have I spilled wine on myself?"

"No. But I have a theory about what's happened since we arrived in Auberon." Selene whispered, looking out through the entryway in case Marek was lurking around.

"And that would be?" Cassie asked.

"I think we're witches." Selene stated.

"Witches…" Cassie scoffed. "You have got to be kidding me."

"Is it so hard to fathom? After everything that's happened recently?" Selene asked.

"Well, yes. I told you before. Witches don't exist. It must just be some kind of side effect of inhaling that smoke earlier. It's messed with us somehow." Cassie theorized.

"No, I don't agree." Selene stated. "I think we were brought together for a reason. I know…" she held up her hands before Cassie could protest. "I consider myself to be a pretty level-headed person, but this entire chain of weird-ass events can't be a coincidence."

"But what if it is?" Cassie asked.

"And what if it isn't?" Selene countered.

Cassie could see the sparkle of excitement in her eyes and she had to admit to that becoming a part of something greater than herself had more appeal than she could say. Yet, there were too many reasons to hesitate. She remained pensive as Selene made them both a martini.

"A penny for your thoughts?" Selene said, sipping her own drink.

Cassie put her glass down and ran her finger around the rim. "Let's just say for a moment, that we're going with your theory that we've been brought here for a reason. Why us? I mean, you probably couldn't have picked three more different women to throw together if you tried."

"True." Selene said, "But variety is the spice of life, as they say."

"Yes, but I mean, have you ever shown any interest in the paranormal, or the occult, witchcraft, anything?" Cassie pressed. "Because I know I haven't."

"Honestly, no. All I wanted was a change. To reclaim my life." Selene said wistfully.

"Same here. That was literally the reason I was at the airport in the first place. I was looking for a fresh start." Cassie confessed.

"So was I." Selene confirmed. "Do you think Addie was too?"

Cassie shrugged, "It seems likely, given how things seem to align between us."

"It's probably not relevant, but the day of our flight was my birthday." Selene said.

"Same here…" Cassie sat up straighter and looked at Selene.

"What's the bet it was Addie's too?" Selene stated.

Cassie just nodded, her mind racing. Despite her rebuttal, she felt hopeful this was more than a coincidence. The sound of a loud car horn interrupted her thoughts as it honked outside.

Cassie raised an eyebrow in distaste. "I take it that's the landlord?"

Selene grinned. "Yes, it seems we've been summoned."

Cassie rolled her eyes as she hopped off the stool and followed Selene out of the kitchen. "Next thing you know, he'll be out there leaning against some ridiculously expensive car all cocky and shit."

Selene giggled, "My soon to be ex-husband drove a ridiculously expensive car."

"My point exactly." Cassie grinned.

They walked out the front and Cassie immediately heard Selene try to stifle a laugh as they found their landlord leaning against a shiny black Audi, looking like he'd stepped out of an advertisement for successful businessmen. Despite the lean, it was clear he was tall, and with his hands folded across his chest, his arm muscles showed that he also worked out.

"He's probably one of those preening gym guys that spends more time admiring themselves in the mirror than they do working out," Cassie thought to herself.

His hair was black, expertly styled, and his clean-shaven face showed off his chiseled jaw. His eyelashes were as dark as his hair and his blue eyes had a mischievous twinkle to them that only made Cassie scowl further. She didn't attempt to hide the look of distaste from her expression—there was nothing she detested more than flashy men. In her opinion, the more money they had, the more obnoxious they seemed to be. He stood up as he saw them, holding out his hand in greeting.

"Selene. Cassie. Nice to meet you. I'm Ravi Saros. Marek told me you went for a bit of a wander around the estate and your friend is missing?"

"Uh, yeah…" Cassie said, frowning. She didn't like the way he seemed so jovial, like a missing person in a strange town was of no consequence.

"I've made some calls, and we've got half the town out looking for her. You need not worry. Though I would suggest the two of you stay inside for the rest of the evening," Ravi said with a broad smile, showing off his immaculate teeth.

"You don't seem concerned that a visitor to your town has just disappeared?" Cassie stated, hearing the accusation in her tone, but not caring.

"I just don't want either of you worrying your pretty little heads over something which I'm sure we'll have rectified by morning. Trust me." Ravi nodded at Marek and opened the door of his car.

"What, that's it?" Cassie asked. "You came all that way just to tell us not to worry about our missing friend?" She felt so infuriated she wanted to reach out and smack him upside the head.

"No. You're right." He slid into the driver's seat and reached over to the passenger's side, before holding out a folder to them. "Lucky you reminded me. Here are the terms for staying at the manor. Fees and payment method are inside, as is some information about where to locate certain amenities throughout the manor. Marek told me money wasn't an issue, is that correct?"

"Uh, yes. That's correct." Selene confirmed, stepping forward and accepting the folder.

"Excellent. The number to my office is inside if you have any questions. Nice to meet you both. Marek, I'll talk to you tomorrow," he said, closing the door and starting the car. Within seconds, he was gone.

"What an absolute…" Cassie was cut off as Selene squeezed her arm.

"He's really not that bad. Once you get to know him." Marek explained.

I find that hard to believe.

"What are we supposed to do now? Addie could be out there wandering around in the cold and we're supposed to just take Ravi's word for it she'll be fine?" Cassie squawked.

"No. Well, yes. I mean…" Marek ran his hand through his tousled blond hair, and Cassie thought she could see a faint flush in his cheeks.

What is he hiding?

"Don't worry about it. We can look after ourselves. Thanks for your help, Marek, and have a good night," Cassie snapped. She grabbed Selene by the hand and pulled her inside, closing the door behind them.

Chapter Seven

Addie

The blasts flew towards her faster, and with more fury; Addie's skin burned from where hot shards of stone had pierced it.

Come on, Addie. You didn't come all this way to have your fanny handed to you by a psychopath. If you think you have powers, now's the time to prove it.

"How much longer do you think you can keep running around in circles, Adamina? There's nowhere for you to go so you may as well surrender," the voice of her pursuer taunted from the other side of the orb, only momentarily out of sight.

He doesn't care if he can't see me. He thinks I'm trapped.

Addie placed her fingers tips on her temples, willing her brain to pull itself together and focus.

What if there was a way out, because I made it so?

Not allowing any room for doubt, Addie placed her hands on the rocky wall and imagined a tunnel. Within seconds, she had to catch herself from falling as the wall before her vanished, leaving in its wake a way out. Addie didn't look back as she darted down the tunnel, hoping to get as far away as she could before he realized she was no longer trapped. Yet she hadn't gotten far when she heard his voice hurtling down the tunnel towards her.

"Two can play at this game, Adamina!"

Suddenly, there were skeletal hands reaching from the walls, pulling at her hair and tugging at her clothing. For every step she took, the number of reaching hands seemed to double until she could hardly move at all. As Addie fought and struggled, her heart thundering in her chest as hot tears of panic pricked her eyes, the man behind her whistled a tune. She yelled in frustration, straining with all her might, but she was stuck.

There was a flash of white light, forcing Addie to close her eyes and turn her head away. When she looked up again an enormous wolf bounded towards her. Her eyes widened as she tried to free herself and get out of its way, but it was no use. As it leaped into the air, Addie squeezed her eyes shut and prayed it would be quick.

She was knocked to the ground, and she groaned in agony for a moment before registering that she was free from the ghoulish hands that had bound her. Pushing herself up onto her elbows, she looked on in awe as the growling creature ripped the hands from their rocky sockets before spitting them across the floor.

"What do you think you're doing here?" The man scowled as he came to a stop about ten feet away from them, his legs shoulder width apart and his fists clenched at his sides.

The wolf growled in response, deep and guttural.

Addie shuffled backwards as quietly as she could, wanting to get as far from both of them as she could. Yet, she also felt compelled to stay. The wolf had freed her.

There's something about its eyes...

The man raised his hands up, a lighting ball forming between his fingertips. The wolf lowered its head to the ground, as though preparing to attack.

There's no way an animal will survive a hit from that thing!

As the man hurtled the ball of lightning towards them, Addie leapt to her feet.

"No!" she yelled, shoving her hand forward. A blast of energy radiated from her palm, like a hazy wall, out over the lowered wolf before expanding and knocking the man off his feet.

Addie let out a whoop of excitement and disbelief as he lay there unmoving.

"I did it?!" she cried, wondering why the wolf still looked so defensive. Her excitement quickly dissipated as the man got to his feet in one swift and inhuman movement.

Oh my goodness…

She staggered backwards, and losing her footing on the rocky floor, fell backwards. Yet instead of the hard terrain, Addie fell onto something soft. Opening her eyes, she found herself on the wolf's back. It raised its head and howled, and Addie threw her arms around its shoulders, holding on for dear life as it hurtled down the tunnel.

Daring to look over her shoulder, Addie saw the man in pursuit, running so fast his legs appeared to be blur—and he was gaining on them.

"Argh!" Addie threw her hand backwards as fiercely as she dared, this time picturing an energy wall of ice. It flew out from her palm and raced towards him, leaving a trail of frost along the tunnel walls as it went. It hit him just as he was preparing another of his lightning balls, freezing him in mid-air. Grinning to herself, she once again clung to the wolf, hoping she'd bought them enough time to get away.

The wolf slowed its pace as the tunnel narrowed all around them, before finally opening again, revealing a smaller cavern. Addie slid off the wolf's back and looked around. "Well, I don't really know how to say thank you to a wolf, but… eek!" she yelped as she turned around to find a man standing where the wolf had been.

"It's okay! I won't hurt you, I promise!" he held up his hand to calm her.

"Are you? Were you? No…" Addie shook her head as she struggled to make sense of what was happening.

"I know. It's a lot. Many people like the idea of shifters, until they actually meet one for real," the man explained, wrapping a frayed piece of cloth around his waist that he seemed to have found on the floor.

"So… you're not a werewolf?" she asked slowly.

He laughed, and despite the ridiculousness of the situation, she smiled at the sound. His dark brown hair was tousled, and he had about a week's worth of stubble on his face. But what really struck were his eyes: Blue, and lined with magnificent laugh lines. Addie felt at ease despite herself.

"Funnily enough, werewolves don't exist anymore than vampires do. Pure fiction," he explained.

"But shifters do," Addie scoffed.

He nodded. "Don't forget about witches and warlocks too."

"Warlock. Is that what he was?" Addie asked, peering over his shoulder towards the tunnel.

"Yes. An ancient, very dangerous, warlock. Which is why we need to get you out of here right now. Your magic won't hold him forever—at least, not yet," he explained as he approached her, placing his hand gently on her back as he guided her to the center of the cavern.

His touch sent shivers up and down her body and it was all she could do to put one foot in front of the other.

"I would love to get out of here. But how?" Addie asked.

"You need to open another portal," he stated, gesturing to the open space before them.

"A portal? Me?" she frowned. "I think perhaps you have the wrong person. I don't know how to do…"

"Yes, you do. You just haven't quite realized it yet. How else do you think you got here in the first place?"

"It was the urn. It did something to me." Addie replied.

"No. You did something to the urn. You created a portal and here you are."

"Huh? But how? I didn't do it intentionally. I wouldn't even know how to go about doing it again." Addie looked at him, wide-eyed.

"You can do it. I will guide you as much as I can, but honestly, the best advice I have is to just not think too much about it. Just let it happen naturally."

"Right. Just let a magical portal appear in a secret tunnel naturally…" Addie said, and he laughed, the sound making her smile once again.

"If it helps, close your eyes. Imagine a portal presenting itself before you. It's small at first, but it soon expands. Envision its ability to take you where you need to go." His voice was soft in her ear and all Addie could think about was their proximity to each other.

"Concentrate…" he whispered.

Addie forced herself to focus on the task at hand.

"That's it. Keep going."

When she felt the vibration beneath her feet, Addie opened her eyes.

"Oh my!" she yelped, throwing her arms around the stranger's neck as she saw the oval portal before her with its swirling teal smoke. Remembering herself, she quickly released him, but the grin on his face let Addie know that he didn't mind.

"You did it! But now you have to go. Hurry!" He started leading her towards the portal, but she pulled him to a stop.

"Wait. I don't even know your name." Addie said, feeling herself blush.

"My name is Jove. Jove Live."

Addie felt her heart skip a beat as he smiled again. "I'm…" The sound of falling rocks within the tunnel interrupted her.

"I know who you are. But now you have to go." Jove stated, his voice now pleading.

"Will I see you again?" Addie asked as she stepped up to the portal.

"I'll make sure of it." Jove said, releasing her.

Addie took a step forward, but before she entered the portal, she quickly stepped back, threw her arms around Jove's neck and kissed him hard on the mouth.

"Thank you," She said, and before he had the chance to respond, she leaped through the portal.

Chapter Eight

Cassie

Cassie rifled through her suitcase where it lay on the floor, making a mess of her belongings as she rummaged around for her favorite pair of jeans. She was certain she'd packed them. Sitting back on the carpet, she sighed, running a hand through her messy blonde hair. Her eyes wandered over to the open closet on the other side of the room; she knew she'd find things with greater ease if she unpacked, yet she really couldn't be bothered. Picturing her sought-after jeans on one of the shelves, Cassie yelped as the suitcase nudged her. Looking down, it seemed to move on its own. From the left corner of the suitcase, her jeans shot up into the air, folding themselves neatly as they approached the wardrobe before landing on the very shelf she'd envisioned.

"Holy shit!" Cassie sat completely still as she stared at the wardrobe. When her heart had stopped pounding, she grinned to herself and sat up straight. Rubbing her hands together, she looked at a pair of black ballet flats. Concentrating, she pictured them on the floor of the wardrobe, and before she could think too much about it, the shoes were in the air and moving into place.

"No way!" Cassie giggled, clapping her hands together.

"You will never believe this!" Cassie bounded into the kitchen in her loose-fitting boyfriend jeans, ballet flats and simple blouse. Selene looked up at her expectantly from where she sat nursing a cup of coffee.

"I've discovered my power!" Cassie declared and bowed dramatically.

"Your weather powers?" Selene asked, with a slight frown.

Cassie rolled her eyes, "No—an actual magical power. Watch." She nodded towards the refrigerator door, and it flew open.

Selene got up from the stool and walked over to the door. She moved it back and forwards with her hand before closing it.

"Do it again," Selene ordered and stood back.

Cassie could hardly contain her excitement as she focused on the door opening, and then watched it happen almost before the thought had even left her mind.

"Okay, yeah. That's pretty cool." Selene smiled.

"Right? I think I might get into this entire witch thing after all," Cassie said. "But on one condition."

"What's that?" Selene asked.

"You conjure me up one of those mugs of coffee too."

Selene rolled her eyes, but laughed as she reached up into the cupboard and withdrew a second mug.

"I wish Addie was here," Cassie said, turning her mug around in circles.

"Yeah, me too. I really hope she's okay. I just don't know what else to do," Selene said.

"Me neither. I mean, it seemed odd the way Ravi seemed so dismissive about it, not to mention the way he was like, oh, don't worry your pretty little heads about it. Ugh. I hate that shit. It makes me so mad!" Cassie exclaimed.

"Yikes! Cassie!" Selene darted off her stool and around to the sink.

Cassie jumped off her own as her coffee mug burst into flames. "Holy shit!" She pushed the mug towards the sink where it toppled in with a loud bang. Selene promptly turned the tap on and doused the fire.

"Woah. That was intense." Selene looked at her with her eyebrows raised.

Cassie nodded slowly. "But awesome, right?"

Selene and Cassie burst into laughter before a loud banging interrupted them.

"What is that?" Selene asked.

"I think it's someone at the front door," suggested Cassie, as the two of them slowly walked out of the kitchen.

"Don't we have a doorbell?" Selene asked in a hushed whisper.

"How should I know?" Cassie asked as they crept towards the door. She stopped a few feet away and held out her arm, gesturing for Selene to stand back. Lifting her other arm up, Cassie slowly moved a finger from left to right and the front door creaked open. The two women peered around, expecting to see someone there, but there was no one. Cassie flicked the rest of the door open.

"What's that?" Selene asked, as she hurried towards a large box sitting on the welcome mat.

From where Cassie stood, she could see that it was wooden, with gold fixtures, and it appeared to have some kind of pattern carved into it. "Careful!" Cassie called out.

"Why? It's not like it's a bomb," Selene said as she picked it up. "Wow, it's heavy!"

Cassie hurried over to help, glancing around for the person who had left it, but there was no sign of anyone.

"Let's take it in here." Cassie led them towards the lounge room, with its art deco lounge complete with day bed, all in teal green.

"Wow, would you look at this room? It looks like it's straight off the set of some old Hollywood movie!" Selene gasped.

"Plenty of time to admire it later, Selene. Right now, I'm curious to see what's in this box. It looks as old as the furniture in here," Cassie said.

"Best not to set them on fire then, hey Cassie?" Selene joked.

"You're hilarious," Cassie said dryly, as they carefully lowered the box onto the coffee table in the middle of the room. They both sat on the lounge and stared at it.

"I think you should open it," Selene finally said.

"Why me?" Cassie asked. "You're the one that wanted to bring it inside."

"I meant you should open it, you know, magically. Besides, it's locked and we don't have a key," Selene explained.

"Oh, yeah. That makes sense." Cassie raised her hands and unlocked the box, then flicked open the latch, before cautiously lifting the lid, listening to it creak with age and disuse. When nothing happened, she let the lid fall open, and they leaned forward for a better look. It was full of something, but there was a piece of velour resting on the top, protecting whatever lay beneath. Taking a deep breath, Cassie grabbed the corners of the material and pulled it away.

"Not what I was expecting," Cassie stated as they looked at a box full of photographs: Very old photographs.

"Me neither. Who are they of?" Selene grabbed a stack and gasped, letting the first one fall from her hand as she quickly inspected the next one, and the next one, her heart pounding away fiercely in her chest.

"This is impossible!" Selene whispered, more to herself than to Cassie.

"What? What is it? I can't see. Who are the photos of?" Cassie asked, leaning forward.

Selene held up one of the larger photographs and turned it around for Cassie to see. "The photographs are of us."

Chapter Nine

Addie

Addie staggered, trying to keep on her feet as she lurched out of the portal. Turning around, she watched it shrink behind her before vanishing completely. She felt a strange pang in her chest as she thought of Jove on the other side. It was crazy, but from the moment Addie had looked into his eyes, she felt like she'd known him forever.

I really hope I see you again. Soon.

Looking around, she saw the urn and sighed with relief. She couldn't wait to get back to the manor and tell Cassie and Selene what had happened. Despite the danger she'd been in, Addie couldn't wipe the smile from her face as she navigated her way back to the bridge. Without a moment's hesitation, Addie traipsed across it, her mind still buzzing with her adventure.

Who was the guy trying to kill me?

How did he know my name?

As she reached the other end of the bridge, Addie's excitement grew. She couldn't recall the last time she'd felt so alive.

Sore from head to toe, but alive.

Weaving her way through the trees, she thought she could hear music drifting towards her. She frowned to herself, wondering where it could be coming from. There was the distinct sound of a clarinet, drums, and a trombone, and Addie realized it was live music—and that it had to be coming from the manor—there was no other property around them for miles.

What is going on? Is there a party? But we don't even know anyone. Weren't they worried about me at all?

Addie reached the last line of trees before the manor gardens and she froze as she saw the garden full of people, drinking and mingling. Stranger still, they were all dressed in old-fashioned clothing. The men wore pinstriped suits with fedora hats or tuxedos, and the women were dressed in an array of sparkling dresses, loaded with sequins and gemstones, some short, some long—all of them with fancy hats or headpieces. Addie stared at them, her mouth agape as she wondered who they were, and where they'd all come from. She scanned the crowd, trying to find Selene or Cassie, but she couldn't see them anywhere.

Surely they wouldn't have left without me?

The tinkling of a spoon against a crystal glass interrupted her thoughts and the music ceased as everyone turned and looked up at the manor's balcony. Standing there was one of the most beautiful women Addie had ever seen, her hair as red as her own, pinned back elegantly. Atop her head was a black, sparkling headband, a brilliant emerald to the side, and plumes of black and green feathers sticking upwards to match her emerald green cocktail dress.

"Can I have your attention, please?" the woman asked, and the murmurings of her guests quickly quieted.

"I wanted to thank you all for coming. It's been an important year for us here, in Auberon, and I couldn't think of a better way to see in the new year, than with all of you. Here's to an afternoon, and evening of wonderful food, marvelous company and even better booze. And here's to a new year to rival the last! Here's to 1920!"

"To 1920!" the crowd cheered, their glasses raised.

What the hell…

Destiny In Danger

Chapter One

Addie

How on earth did I end up in 1920?

Addie stared up at the red-haired woman on the balcony as she raised her glass to the crowd below before taking a sip.

This cannot be happening.

Keeping close to the tree line, Addie snuck around the perimeter of the garden, her heart pounding in her chest as she tried to make sure she stayed out of the view of the guests. Fortunately, they all seemed far too engrossed in their tipsy banter to pay any attention to a woman from the future lurking in the forest.

Addie paused and looked up at the balcony again and watched as the woman turned and disappeared back into the manor. While she had no idea who that woman was, or how she had ended up jumping into the past, Addie was certain that woman would know something.

At least I sure hope so.

Addie kept as close as she could to the manor without breaking from the tree lines while she tried to look for a way to get inside the manor without being seen. While Addie was known for her taste in vintage attire, the dress she wore was more akin to the 1950s and she was bound to stand out if she tried to casually make her way through the crowd. As she was about to concede that she might have to hide in the trees until the evening, a band stepped onto a small stage set up on the opposite end of the garden. All the guests turned as a voluptuous woman in a sparkling cocktail dress and a magnificent feathered headpiece stepped up to the microphone and crooned a jazzy melody. With the crowds backs to her hiding place, Addie seized the opportunity and dashed out of the woods, keeping close to the edge of the manor before slipping in through the open French doors. She startled a waitress as she entered, who was fortunately more concerned with trying to stop the glasses from toppling off her tray than inspecting Addie. Muttering her apologies, Addie hurried through the kitchen, around into the foyer and towards the grand staircase. There were numerous waitstaff milling about, carrying trays of sparkling wine and fancy little canapes, and were thankfully too focused on their own tasks to pay her any attention.

Addie reached the staircase, stepped up onto the first railing and placed her hand on the curved wooden banister. As soon as she gripped the railing, she was overcome with a vision. It was only brief, but she saw herself on the second floor and opening a closed door. On the other side was the woman, her hand outstretched as though beckoning her. Opening her eyes, Addie knew she was on the right track—the woman had to hold the answers she was looking for. She hurried up the stairs, ignoring the burning of her leg muscles as she ran, knowing she was not the most athletic of women, and she reached the landing with a grateful huff, pausing for a moment to catch her breath. Looking along the corridor, first left and then right, Addie stared at the identical doors and tried to recall which one she went through in the vision. As her eyes fell upon the second door to her right, she could swear it appeared illuminated, as though there was a bright light pushing through the gaps around the door. Taking it as a sign, Addie hurried over to it and grasped the doorknob with her hand. As she twisted, she'd half-expected to find it locked, and felt surprised when the door cracked open. It slowly swung open, revealing a grand room, and Addie gasped at the sight of it. It was a vast room—at least by Addie's standards—and looked like a personal library. On the other side of the room stood the woman she'd seen on the balcony addressing the guests. She had her back to Addie, and appeared to be staring out a large, circular window. The music from the band below drifted up towards them as Addie took a hesitant step into the room. When the woman didn't move, Addie ambled forward, her hands clasped before her as she looked around in awe. Oak bookshelves lined the walls on either side of the room, laden with a combination of books and ornaments. The top shelves were lined with jars which appeared to contain dried herbs, flowers and seeds—though a few jars contained some rather ominous looking items Addie couldn't identify. The plush, cream carpet absorbed the sound of her footsteps and she wondered if the woman was so engrossed in the music from below that she hadn't heard her come in. Not wanting to startle her, Addie thought it best to announce herself.

"Excuse me? Hello?" Addie said, peering at the woman for any sign that she'd heard her. As the woman slowly turned and looked at her, Addie gasped, her hands flying over her mouth.

She looks exactly like me!

Chapter Two

Selene

"This makes no sense at all." Cassie said, flicking from one photograph to another.

Selene picked another up from the box and shook her head. "How is it even possible?"

"It's not, right?" Cassie frowned. "I mean, according to the back of this photograph, it's dated in 1890. So obviously, it's not us. It must just be some kind of strange coincidence."

Selene leaned back as she looked from the box of photographs, to Cassie and back again. "Look, I get that you're the smart one of our little group, and I'm fine with that. But if I can see there is something more than a coincidence going on here, surely you can too?"

"Yes... I know." Cassie groaned. "It's just, I've always been the type of person who has to see something to believe it, you know? But this is ridiculous. I'm looking at these photographs with my own two eyes and I can't believe it for a second. I mean, it's just not possible. Is it?"

Selene shrugged. "You already said that."

"Well, what are your thoughts then?" Cassie asked.

"I don't know what to say. I'm right there with you—I know what I'm seeing, yet I can't make any sense of it. It's one thing to see an old photograph of an ancestor and see a resemblance, but I *know* these aren't our ancestors. And they look just like us. I think that's the bit I'm struggling with the most."

"You mean aside from the fact we only met a couple of days ago and now we find vintage photos with our doppelgängers in them?" Cassie said with a rueful smile.

"There is also that." Selene replied with a sigh.

They sat in silence for a moment, each of them lost in their own thoughts as they stared at women in the photographs.

"Okay, let's see if we can simplify this some way. What do we know so far?" Cassie started. "We know these women look like us…"

"Exactly like us…" Selene cut in.

Cassie nodded. "But it's obviously not us, because where here. Now."

"Right. I'm with you so far." Selene agreed.

"Good. Now, I know you said they aren't our ancestors, but what if they are, and we just never knew about them?" Cassie suggested. "I mean, that really is the only logical explanation I can think of why they look like us."

Selene scrunched her face. "I think there's a difference between looking like someone and looking exactly like someone. Besides, what are the odds of the three of us looking like three women in the same photo? Even if we're related somewhere down the line, those odds are just insane."

Cassie sighed and tossed the photographs into the box. "I have no idea. I can't explain it. Three women from as far back as two hundred years ago that looked exactly like us. Only we're almost certain that the three of us aren't related, and until a couple of days ago, you, me and Addie were complete strangers. I don't know about you, but I'm fairly certain that's the craziest shit I've ever heard."

"Oh, I don't know… three women who were previously strangers arriving in a small town and discovering they've miraculously developed magical powers must be up there?" Selene grinned.

"Well, when you put it like that…" Cassie giggled.

"Maybe we're just looking at this the wrong way." Selene suggested.

"How else can we look at it?" Cassie asked, massaging her neck with her hand.

"Well, what if someone left this box of photographs at the front door for an entirely different reason and we're just getting distracted with appearances?" Selene suggested, watching Cassie, who appeared to consider it before shaking her head.

"Great, now we've just added to our list of unanswered questions." Cassie sighed. "But what reason could someone have to bring these to us?"

"Maybe we're supposed to work out who these women were. Like a mystery or something." Selene suggested.

"I think you're enjoying all this chaos and confusion way too much." Cassie smiled.

"Well," Selene smiled back, "Until the moment I stepped onto the plane with you and Addie, my life was so boring. It was all charity galas and restaurants and hosting and premiers…"

"Wow, you're right, that sounds totally mundane, it must have been awful for you." Cassie rolled her eyes.

"You don't understand. No one cared what I thought, or what I wanted. My family didn't care that I didn't want to marry my husband, because all they cared about was the prestige it would add to their name, and the added opportunities that came with that. My husband didn't care that I didn't love him, because he wanted a trophy to display, a reason for his friends to slap him on his back and tell him he'd done well for himself. Everything was about keeping up appearances, but not actually living." Selene stated, her eyes on the carpet beneath them.

"I'm sorry, Selene. I feel like such a jerk. I shouldn't have jumped to conclusions. What made you leave it all behind? I imagine that would've been a scary decision to make." Cassie said.

"It was, and it wasn't. I had a health scare a couple of months ago. I found a lump in my breast. They tested it, and I'm fine, but going through that I realized I had no one to turn to, no one that cared enough to even recognize that I was going through something stressful. Before I got the all clear, I just kept asking myself what I had to show for my life—and the answer kept coming back as nothing. I'd lived my entire life pleasing everyone else. So, while it was scary deciding to walk away from it all, I knew staying meant death, at least of one kind or another."

They sat quietly for a moment before Cassie spoke. "Though I'm sure being worth a fortune in your own right helps when venturing out into the big wide world."

"Yeah, there's also that." Selene replied and looked up at Cassie before the two of them burst into laughter.

Suddenly, there was a thud from behind them, and they exchanged a quick glance before getting to their feet.

"What was that?" Cassie asked as Selene scanned the room on the other side of the couch. On the carpet, about a meter away from the bookshelf, lay an ornament.

"That wasn't on the floor before, was it?" Selene asked.

Cassie shook her head as she hurried over to it and picked it up for a closer look. She frowned as she held it up to Selene. It was a bronze statue of an owl, with his its wings semi-raised, as though it was about to spread them and fly off. It had a small, curved and pointy beak, with round eyes made of red stones.

"Are they… are they rubies?" Selene asked in awe as she gently reached out and touched them.

"How would I know? That seems like it's more up your ally than mine." Cassie scoffed.

"I think they are, which is crazy. They'd have to be the size of a coin… these would be worth a small fortune." Selene gasped.

"Are you really that surprised? Are you not staying in the same manor that I am?" Cassie asked.

Selene didn't answer as she continued to inspect the statue.

"What I'm interested to know is how something that heavy just falls on the floor." Before Cassie could elaborate any further, they heard a slow creaking sound coming from the front of the house. "Was that…"

"… the front door?" Selene finished for her, and the two of them scurried from the lounge room, huddled together. As they reached the foyer and saw the front door wide open, they froze.

"Hello?" Cassie called out, "Anyone here?"

Selene gripped Cassie's arm, not sure which would be worse—to hear a response or not. When there wasn't one, Cassie stepped forward. "Stuff this." As she got within reaching distance of the front door, it suddenly slammed closed.

Selene yelped as Cassie froze in place. "What the hell…"

Selene trudged up to Cassie and rubbed her back, more trying to reassure herself than anyone else, and before she could second guess herself, she stepped forward and yanked the front door back open. Cassie joined her as the two of them peered outside, looking for any sign of a prankster.

"Maybe it was the wind." Selene suggested.

"That would be a fine theory if there was any. It's as still as anything today." Cassie added.

The sound of a car coming up the driveway interrupted them, and seconds later Marek's jeep appeared. Selene felt her mouth go dry as she watched him expertly swing the jeep around the circular driveway and pull up in front of them.

Marek jumped out of the car and walked around to them. "Good afternoon, ladies." He said with a charming smile, his blue eyes twinkling as he ran his hands through his scruffy blond hair.

"Hey, Marek." Cassie said.

Selene just gave a small nod, finding herself unable to talk.

What the hell is wrong with you? You don't get like this with guys, now snap out of it! It's not like he's even your type. Wait... do I even have a type?

"Did you see anyone else on your way up to the house?" Cassie asked.

Marek frowned, shaking his head. "No, I didn't. Why? Is everything okay?"

"Oh yeah, no dramas, I was curious is all."

"Speaking of curious, what is that?" he asked, pointing to the owl statue still in Cassie's hands.

"Oh! We're just checking out some of the magnificent pieces around the manor." Selene blurted out. "Cassie likes owls."

"Uh, yes. I do. What can we do for you?" Cassie replied.

"Uh, I was actually wondering if Selene would like to join me for a drink in town." Marek looked at Selene and she scowled as the heat of a blush spread across her cheeks. Despite his smile, there was an intensity to his gaze that both frightened and excited her—and she didn't know which she was more afraid of. Before she could say anything, Cassie was pushing her forward.

"That sounds like a lovely idea! She'd love to go, wouldn't you, Selene?"

"Uh, what about…" Selene started.

"There's nothing that can't wait until later. Go enjoy yourselves." Cassie insisted, almost pushing Selene into Marek.

"I don't think it's a very good idea for you to be here on your own, I mean, we still don't know what's happened to Addie…" Selene hesitated.

"Don't be ridiculous. I'm a grown-ass woman and I can look after myself. If it makes you feel any better, I'll be sure to lock the doors once you leave." Cassie assured her.

Selene stared at Cassie, her eyebrow raised, but Cassie was either oblivious to her annoyance, or more likely, choosing to ignore it.

Marek opened the passenger side door for her, and Selene conceded that she had no choice but to go, and she avoided meeting his eyes as she climbed up into the car.

"Have fun!" Cassie waved enthusiastically as Marek strode around to the driver's side.

Selene scowled at Cassie through the window, but that only seemed to make her grin even more. Marek climbed into the driver's seat and turned to her, his smile setting a flurry of butterflies alight in her stomach.

"Ready?" he asked, sticking the key into the ignition.

Selene could only nod, not trusting herself to speak again as a wave of nerves took over.

Marek started the car and steered them back down the driveway as Selene pretended to be enthralled with the scenery.

Oh my, he smells amazing… This guy will be the death of me.

Chapter Three

Addie

The woman stared back at her, not appearing to be in the least bit surprised to find Addie standing there—or by the fact they looked exactly alike.

What is happening? This can't be real; I must be hallucinating or something.

"I assure you, you're not." The woman spoke.

Addie's mouth fell open. "You read my mind?"

"I did." The woman replied matter-of-factly as she gracefully moved away from the window and walked over to one of two identical chaise chairs facing each other on the right side of the room. The woman took a seat and leaned against the cushions, looking like a glamourous actress right out of old Hollywood. Addie could only stand there with her mouth open until the woman gestured with her hand for Addie to join her. Addie walked over to the opposite chair and sat down on the plush burgundy velvet. She felt like she was experiencing déjà vu, but she knew that couldn't be possible. It felt surreal looking at her doppelganger and she looked at anything and everything else except the woman, though she could feel her eyes on her as she silently watched her. Addie stared at the shelves, close enough now to inspect the rows of old books, intricate crystals of all shapes and sizes and the large glass jars. She felt intrigued by some of the more unusual looking contents, and while all the jars were neatly labelled, she still couldn't read them from where she sat. Her gaze drifted over to a framed portrait on the adjoining wall behind the woman, and Addie got to her feet before she even realized what she was doing. She could feel the woman's eyes on her as she moved, but they both remained silent. Lifting her hand to her mouth, Addie stared at the old sepia photograph, framed in a simple wooden frame on the wall. The photograph was of three women standing side by side, their hands clasped in front of them. They wore severe, high-necked black dresses, with full sleeves and long skirts that brushed the tops of their buttoned black boots. Yet, as Addie forced herself to look at their faces, she knew what she would see. The women were herself, Selene and Cassie. Her eyes looked down to the bottom right-hand corner where the image was dated 1850.

This can't be.

"Of course, it can. It is." The woman said.

"Will you stop reading my mind?" Addie snapped as she turned away from the painting. "It's rude." Addie stormed back over to the chair and sat before quickly standing back up again, her hands on her hips.

"Look, I'm sorry for sneaking into the manor. I'm not supposed to be here—like, literally not supposed to be here, in 1920. But something tells me you can help me get back to… well, my time." Addie declared.

The woman looked up at her. "What makes you say that?"

Addie raised her eyebrows. "Let's see. There's the fact you can read my mind, the fact you have all this weird stuff on your shelves, there's that photograph on the wall and you're not in the least bit surprised to see me. Oh, and there's also the tiny detail that you look exactly like me. Who are you, anyway?"

The woman leaned forward, resting her elbow elegantly across her knees. "My name is Adamina Naya."

Addie opened her mouth and closed it again, letting the words sink in. The woman just watched her until she could finally speak. "That is not possible. I'm Adamina Naya. You can't be me—this is 1920…"

"I am you. I'm also not you. It's a little complex and not the easiest thing to explain…" the woman started.

"Well, how about you try?" Addie demanded.

"First, I'm intrigued to know where are you from? As in what year?"

"2020." Addie replied. Despite the woman saying she was intrigued, in actuality, she seemed more focused on her fingernails than by Addie's answer. "You know what's happening, don't you? To me and my friends?"

"I know it's frustrating," the woman finally looked up, "but I can't tell you anything. You and your friends need to uncover your path for yourselves. If you try to unravel your path sooner than you're meant to, then the consequences could be dire. Catastrophic, even."

Before Addie could respond, there came a crashing sound from outside, followed by screams. Addie and the woman dashed over to the window and looked out. There was an extensive section at the forest's edge that stood blackened and singed with golden embers snaking up what remained of the trees. Smoke blew up towards the windows, making it hard initially for either women to see what was going on, yet as the screaming intensified, Addie knew it was nothing good.

"How did you come to be here?" The woman asked in a hushed voice, placing her hand against the windowpane as though it would somehow help her see better.

"Uh, through a portal. I was down in a cavern being chased by…"

"Brenner…" the woman gasped as the smoke cleared and they could see the chaos below.

"That's him!" Addie cried as they saw the man below, hurling fiery orbs at the party goers below.

"Didn't you lock the portal behind you?" The woman turned and asked her.

"Huh?" was all Addie could say.

The woman sighed and grabbed Addie by the arm and pulled her away from the window. "You have to lock the portal behind you, especially if you're being pursued by someone—or something—you don't want to follow you. You led him straight to us."

"You know that man?" Addie asked as she let herself get pulled into the middle of the room.

"Unfortunately, yes, though it has been some time since we've gone head to head. He's an evil warlock of the worst kind. He's supposed to be forever banished from this realm. It should have been impossible for him to return." The woman said rapidly as she turned her head toward the window as the house shook under the weight of some kind of explosion, followed by further screams.

"You must leave before it's too late. If he finds us both here, together, the consequences would be astronomical." The woman stopped and lifted a chain that hung around her neck, revealing a key attached to it she'd hidden within her dress. "Take this." She placed the key and chain into the palm of Addie's hand and wrapped her fingers over it. "You need to create another portal if you want to get out of here. I will try to buy you as much time as I can."

A crashing sound came from below, within the house, and the woman pulled Addie into a tight embrace. "Take care of each other. For all our sakes." Releasing Addie, the woman turned and hurried out of the room, pulling the door shut behind her.

"Wait! I don't think I can create another portal!" Addie called out, but the door remained closed. Addie looked around frantically, not knowing where to start as the crashing and screaming moved through the house beneath her, while outside seemed eerily quiet. Her thoughts suddenly diverted to Jove in the cavern and how he'd helped her create the last portal. She felt a flutter in her chest at the recollection.

Addie Naya! Now is not the time!

Holding out her hands before her, she tried to focus on those feelings and use them as energy to create a new portal. She closed her eyes, trying to block out the violent sounds rapidly approaching, and when she opened them, Addie gasped when she saw it forming before her. It moved slowly at first, but quickly expanded the more she focused on it. There was a large crashing sound from the hallway and several jars and books fell from the shelves, crashing to the floor around her, but Addie held her focus. As soon as it was large enough, Addie crossed her fingers and leaped through it. The last thing she heard were the sounds of the woman screaming.

Chapter Four

Cassie

With her back against the closed front door, Cassie listened to the sound of Marek's car leaving. She felt grateful to have some time to herself to absorb everything that was happening—and do a little more digging on her own. Looking down at the owl in her hand, she turned it over, wondering how it could have possibly come off the shelf. Cassie decided it warranted further investigation, and she walked back over to the bookshelf in the living room. It didn't take long to see its resting place, due to the dust-free circle left exposed. Cassie put it back and ran her hands over the edge of the shelf. As far as she could tell, it was straight, so she didn't think it had somehow slid off. She poked it with her forefinger, trying to determine how much force it would take to expel it onto the ground. When it didn't move, she pushed it with her palm, and only then did it topple back to the ground. Cassie stared down at its ruby-red eyes as though they were in a standoff, before she picked it up and put it back on the shelf.

Like everything else that was happening around them, Cassie had no explanation for what had happened, and she resolved herself to dealing with one issue at a time. Walking over to where they'd left the photos, Cassie sat on the rug beside the box. She picked up a bunch and started flicking through them again, slowly shaking her head.

This is so bizarre. These women look exactly like us—how will that ever make any sense.

As she continued to flick through them, Cassie noticed there were several of them taken in the same room. Peering at the images, she thought the room looked like it was part of the manor and yet; it didn't look like any of the room she'd seen so far. Holding a slightly larger photograph up for a closer look, Cassie inspected the image of three women again, looking exactly like herself, Selene and Addie. In this image they were dressed in vintage dresses with feathered headpieces, and long pearl necklaces. She initially thought they might have been dressed up for a themed party, but when she turned the photo over, the date was

New Year's Eve, 1920. The three women sat together on a beautiful-looking chaise lounge as they posed, unsmiling, at the camera. Cassie thought the image looked like it belonged in some vintage Vogue magazine. Forcing herself to focus on looking for clues, she noted there was a bookshelf along the wall to their left—only partially in shot. Just enough so that Cassie could see it contained books and what looked like some large crystal clusters—but the rest of it was excluded from the shot. Over to the right side of the photograph, Cassie could see the last third of a circular window, and she frowned as she looked at it.

I would recall seeing a circular window in the manor—wouldn't I?

Scrambling to her feet, Cassie jogged towards the front door and pulled it open. She continued to the other side of the driveway before turning and looking up at the manor. Scanning the building, she concluded there were no circular windows like in the picture. She ran back inside, closing the door behind her, and jogged through to the other side of the house and out into the garden. Looking up at the house she again could only see the large rectangular windows that she'd seen from the front.

But I'm sure those photographs are from within the manor. More damn questions and no answers!

Frowning to herself, Cassie strode back into the house, but as she was about to enter the living room again, she heard the creak of the front door open.

Don't tell me that's Selene back already. Poor Marek.

Yet, as she walked out into the foyer, there was no one there. As she stared at the open door, her heart skipped a beat and she questioned whether it had been such a smart idea to stay in the manor on her own.

Don't be ridiculous. Get it together, Cassie. You probably didn't close it properly when you came back inside. You were in too much of a hurry to find a stupid window that doesn't exist.

As she reached out to close the door, a loud bang sounded from behind her, causing her to jump.

"Oh, come on!" Cassie yelled, more annoyed than scared, and she stormed back into the lounge room. On the middle of the floor was an enormous book, and she looked at it curiously.

Surely that can't be responsible for such a loud bang?

Cassie walked over and went to pick it up, surprised to find it weighed a ton. She needed both hands to retrieve it and was stunned to find that the cover of the book was made from a thick metal. She opened the book up to find the pages towards the back were glued together, and a small section was cut out of the middle, resulting in a little hiding place. Only it was empty.

Swearing under her breath, Cassie closed the book and looked for the place on the shelves it had come from.

Well, I'll be damned…

Standing on her tiptoes, Cassie peered up at the gap between two books. On the sliver of wall left exposed by the missing book, was an old iron lock.

I wonder what's on the other side.

Chapter Five

Selene

Marek tried to make conversation as he and Selene drove toward town by asking Selene a couple of questions to which she only responded with single-syllable answers. Selene felt like all the charm and social skills she'd relied on her whole life had vanished, leaving her feeling self-conscious and nervous—two feelings that were entirely foreign to her.

You're being rude. Poor Marek is just making conversation.

Deciding to change track, Selene thought by asking Marek the questions, he'd be forced to do most of the talking.

"Do you have a girlfriend?" she blurted, groaning inwardly as soon as the words left her mouth.

What the hell is wrong with you?

Marek flashed her a quick look, his eyebrows raised, before he burst out laughing. "Direct. I can appreciate that. The answer is no, I do not have a girlfriend."

"Oh." Selene replied, swallowing thickly.

There was a brief silence before Marek elaborated. "I did have. We'd been together since high school and I thought she was the one. That was, until I found out she cheated on me. Repeatedly. I've been single since."

"I'm sorry, that's awful." Selene turned and looked at him, wanting to reach out and touch his arm, but forced herself to maintain restraint. "So that was fairly recent then?"

Marek shook his head. "It was a couple of years ago now."

"What?" Selene yelped before instantly regretting it. "I'm sorry, I didn't mean to sound…I don't know…that just seems like a long time to be single for someone so…so…"

"So?" Marek prompted and Selene felt her face flush, knowing she'd backed herself into a corner. "I just meant you seem really…nice."

Marek grinned at her, sending her heart in a flutter. "Nice. I can take that. I think you seem nice too."

"Really?" Selene asked incredulously and Marek erupted in laughter.

"Well, you're a little prickly and not the easiest person to get to know, but what can I say? I'm up for the challenge."

Selene placed her hand over her mouth while she stared out the window, trying to hide her smile. She felt like a giddy schoolgirl around him, which annoyed her, and the constant butterflies she felt in his proximity made her feel nauseas. Even without looking at him, she couldn't escape the way their closeness made her feel. It was like every part of her felt electrified and on edge—though it wasn't unpleasant. It was exciting—and scary.

Stop it. He must be at least ten years younger than you! You're being ridiculous. Besides, there are far more important things to focus on.

What unnerved Selene most of all, was that she was used to being in control. Calm. Collected. Yet when she was around Marek, she felt anything but. It was all she could do not to sigh with relief when he finally pulled the jeep up in front of the pub. She actually hoped there were other patrons inside, so she wouldn't feel so alone with him. Marek got out of the car and Selene almost fell out in her hurry to get out before he could open the door for her. Instead, she ended up falling straight into his arms. She looked up into his eyes, surprised by how blue they were up close—like a cloudless, afternoon sky. Marek grinned at her and her heart felt like it was doing somersaults in her chest. Clearing her throat, Selene righted herself and pulled away before putting some distance between them. Marek just continued to smile as he waived his arm out before him, gesturing for her to lead the way.

As soon as Selene opened the door, she felt repulsed by the smell of stale beer and fried food but felt determined not to stand out like a sore thumb. Sure, it was nothing like the five-star restaurants and glitzy venues she was used to frequenting, but she reminded herself the whole reason she'd taken a trip in the first place was because she wanted a change of scene.

Can't get much more of a change of scene than this.

Once inside the pub, Selene hovered, unsure what to do next. She almost jumped out of her skin as she felt

Marek's hand on the small of her back, and she looked up at him in surprise.

Wow, he really is tall. How did I not notice that before? And the way his blond hair always looks like he's just run his hands through it. I know I'd like to…

"What would you like to drink?" he asked her, and she felt her face flush.

"Uh, yes. I'll have a glass of prosecco, please." Selene replied, diverting her gaze from his face.

"Sure. Why don't you choose somewhere to sit, and I'll bring the drinks over?" Marek suggested and Selene gave a quick nod as she eyed off the empty booths along the far wall. Deciding she didn't think she could handle sharing the secluded quarters with Marek, she opted for a small table closest to them. Selene went to tuck her handbag under her chair, but quickly thought better of it and placed it on her lap. While she waited, she looked around at the pub which was far quieter than the first time she'd stepped—barefoot—inside it. It was strange, but it almost felt like a lifetime ago that she'd stood near the steps with Addie and Cassie. She smiled as she thought how much her life had changed since meeting them, and for the first time in her life she felt like she had genuine friends, not just people interested in her money or her husband's status.

If only they could see me now, sitting in a pub with a handsome younger man, with two new friends and magical powers to boot.

"They didn't have any prosecco, so I got you a glass of white wine instead. Something called Sauvignon Blanc. I'm not really up on what makes an excellent wine, so I hope that's okay?" Marek asked as he placed the glass on the table in front of her.

Selene gave him a quick smile and thanked him.

Just as he placed his beer on the table, his phone rang and he pulled it from his back pocket and inspected the screen. "I'm sorry, I have to take this. Do you mind?"

Selene shook her head. "Not at all."

He flashed her a smile that caused her heart to flutter in her chest and strode away, leaving Selene with her wine.

Hold on, how is his phone working when ours won't? I thought he said there was no reception in Auberon.

She turned around, but Marek was already outside on the footpath, his phone pressed to his ear. She frowned as she watched him and knew she would have to ask him about it when he returned. In the meantime, she turned back around and picked up her glass of wine. Taking a sip, Selene tried to hide her grimace before she placed the glass back on the table. Her distaste quickly evaporated though as she recalled her newly acquired talent. Grinning to herself, Selene flashed a quick glance around the half empty pub. The bartender had his back to her as he restocked the bar. There were a couple of guys with beers watching a sports match on a large television on the far wall, and another man slouched in the corner booth, hunched over as though he'd already had too much to drink.

Good. No one's paying any attention to me.

She rubbed her hands together quickly and then placed her fingertips on the wineglass. Watching intently, she willed the wine to change into the prosecco she craved, and it was all she could do not to erupt into a fit of giggles as the tiny bubble started rising from the bottom of the glass. Selene picked up the glass and took another sip. This time she closed her eyes, the bubbles tickling the tip of her nose as she enjoyed the crisp flavour of apple, melon and pear.

This has got to be the best prosecco I've ever tasted.

She was pulled from her thoughts as Marek sat opposite her. "Sorry about that, it was a work call."

"Not a problem at all." Selene said, "Question, though. How come your phone works when ours don't? I thought you said there's no reception here?"

"Uh, it's a, uh, most don't. Work provides me with a phone that can pick up reception so they can reach me." He explained.

"What, like a satellite phone or something?" she asked.

"Yeah, pretty much." Marek took a swig of his beer before placing it back on the table. Selene nodded but she noticed the way he didn't look at her as he answered, flicking his gaze to the beer in front of him, to the street and back again.

But why would he lie?

Selene picked up her own glass of wine and took a delicate sip, distracted momentarily as she savoured the taste.

"What's that?" Marek asked, pointing at her glass, a slight frown marring his features.

"Oh! Turns out they had my drink after all." Selene replied with a shrug that she hoped was casual, and she made a point of his meeting his stare, as though daring him to challenge her.

Marek looked around the pub, his gaze lingering on the guy in the booth before he turned back around without a word and took a big gulp of beer. "So, how are you liking Auberon?" he finally asked.

"It's been… interesting so far." she replied before she could stop herself.

"Yeah? How so?"

"Oh, it's hard to explain. It's just been different than what I'm used to, staying with two other women I just met in a place I'd never heard of before. It sure is beautiful here though."

"That it is. So, you didn't know Cassie and Addie before now? I just assumed the three of you were friends." Marek asked.

"We are." Selene said in their defence. "It's just we hadn't met before we ended up on the same plane together. It was all by chance."

"Was it?" Marek asked and the sudden change in the tone of his voice made her look up, but he smiled as soon as she did.

Before Selene could respond, a sleek, black cat leaped up onto the table. It turned its back to Selene and faced Marek, meowing loudly. She watched as Marek lowered his beer, his eyes fixed firmly on the cat as the creature continued to meow. Selene frowned as she watched the spectacle.

If I didn't know any better, I'd think they were communicating with each other.

Marek stood up so quickly his chair toppled over, but he made no move to pick it up—his eyes still fixed on the cat.

"Marek?"

He ignored her as he looked over his shoulder to the booth that was now empty.

"We have to leave. Now." he stated.

Selene's eyes widened as the cat appeared to nod at him, before it jumped off the table and ran off across the pub. "What do you mean? We just got here?"

"I said now." Marek grabbed her arm and Selene just managed to grasp her handbag, stopping it from falling to the ground. As she was pulled to her feet, she knocked against the table, sending her glass of wine toppling to the floor where it shattered. Yet Marek didn't look back as he led them from the pub and out onto the street. He only released her to open the passenger door of the jeep.

"Marek, what…"

"Get in. Hurry." Marek looked over his shoulder as he waited for her to get in.

"No! I will do no such thing until you tell me what is going on!" Selene snapped, folding her arms angrily across her chest. If there was one thing she hated, it was being told what to do.

"Selene, we don't have time…"

"Make time!" Selene demanded. "You invited me out for a drink, then as soon as we get here, you take a call when you told us there was no reception here—and FYI I know what a satellite phone looks like, and that's not one."

Marek opened his mouth like he was going to try and argue the point, but seemed to think better of it.

"Then, you come back inside and have a moment with a cat before dragging me out on the street. What the hell? Were you talking to that cat in there?" Selene snapped.

"Don't be ridiculous…" Marek started before Selene cut him off.

"Don't call me ridiculous! I know what I saw, so if you want to see me again, then do me the courtesy of telling me the truth, rather than trying to make out like I'm the crazy one in attempt to divert my attention."

"You're right. I'm sorry. That wasn't fair." Marek said, his eyes wide and filled with a sudden sadness that caused a pang in Selene's chest. She wanted to reach out and grab his hand, to apologize for yelling at him, but Selene stopped herself. Her desire for the truth was stronger.

"It's just, things are different here in Auberon, to what you're used to." Marek said quietly.

"How so?" Selene asked.

Does he know about us? About out powers?

Marek cleared his throat. "Selene, believe me when I tell you we don't have time to get into right now, but I promise you, I will tell you everything once you let me get us out of here. You're too exposed."

"No. I want to know now…" Selene was silenced as Marek stepped forward and placed his hands on either side of her face as he bent down and kissed her.

The moment their lips touched, Selene's heart pounded furiously against her chest and she felt a tingle course through her whole body. Without thinking about it, she reached up and wrapped her arms around his neck as their kiss deepened. When he pulled away, Selene felt every part of her cry out in protest.

"Please, Selene. I need you to trust me. We can talk about this more but I need you to get in…"

He was cut off as an enormous man suddenly appeared at the front of the jeep. Selene screamed, and Marek pushed her behind him. She peered around him at the man who stood at least a head taller than Marek, and twice as wide. He was dressed in black from head to toe and wore a hooded cape. She couldn't see much of his face from beneath it, but from what she could see, his skin was bone white and his lips appeared cracked and bloody.

A guttural groan came from him, but Marek cast his hand in the man's direction and sent him flying half-way down the street.

"How did you?" Selene stammered, but Marek scooped her up in his arms and placed her in the passenger seat before she could protest again.

"Put your seatbelt on." he commanded before slamming the door shut and running around to the other side of the car. Starting the engine, he pulled out into the street. A car horn honked loudly behind them, but Marek didn't even acknowledge it as he sped towards the man who was slowly getting to his feet in the middle of the road.

"Marek! You're headed straight for him!" Selene screamed, gripping the armrest to steady herself as she flicked sideways glances at Marek. He didn't seem to hear her, focused instead on the man as he pressed the accelerator to the floor. The man was now on his feet and spread his arms out to the sides as a deep howl came from him that sent a chill up Selene's spine. It looked like he was daring them to hit him.

"Marek!" Selene screamed again, bracing herself for impact by placing her free hand on the roof over her head. She squeezed her eyes shut and turned her head—but nothing happened. When she opened her eyes, the man had disappeared, and they were still hurtling down the street.

She lowered her arm and turned to Marek, her mouth open and her eyes wide. "Wh... where did he go?"

"He's gone for now. But he'll be back. He knows who you are now." Marek answered, not taking his eyes off the road.

"People don't just disappear into thin air." Selene scoffed.

"Yeah, sometimes they do." Marek stated, his voice tight.

"And what do you mean, he knows who I am now? Seriously, who was that guy and how did he just appear like that?"

Marek opened his mouth as though to answer, before closing it again, staring at her a moment before looking in the review mirror instead.

"You said you would tell me what's going on!" Selene snapped.

"Just let me get you back to the manor. Then we'll talk." Marek declared, his eyes fixed either on the road before them, or on the review mirror.

"Are you expecting us to be followed?" Selene asked, but he didn't answer. She shook her head, playing back what had just happened, and unsuccessfully trying to make sense of it all.

Once they turned off the main road and started up the winding road to the manor, Marek seemed to relax slightly and finally broke his silence. "I need you to tell me what happened at the pub."

"Huh? What are you talking about? You were there." Selene frowned.

"While I was outside. What did you do?" Marek asked.

Selene gaped at him unable to answer at first.

Shit. Does he know? I'm such an idiot using my powers. The girls are going to kill me.

"What are you talking about? You're the one you dragged us out of the pub like the place was on fire.

What did *you* do?" Selene didn't like the stormy expression on his face, as though the danger hadn't passed, and it made her feel fearful.

He flashed a couple of quick looks in her direction before answering. "It was your drink, wasn't it? They didn't replace your drink, did they? You did."

Selene opened her mouth to refute his accusation, but the hurt look he shot her way stopped her.

"I can only protect you if you're honest with me, otherwise you're just putting us—and your friends in danger." Marek said quietly, his eyes fixed firmly on the road.

It's not just my secret to tell. It wouldn't be fair for me to tell him without speaking to Addie and Cassie first. But what if I'm—we're—in danger?

"Well?" Marek snapped and Selene could only look at him, her eyes wide and she noticed for the first time how tense he looked, semi-hunched over the steering wheel, his knuckles white. It made her feel guilty and she sighed softly before answering.

"What would you say if I told you I did replace my own drink—with magic?" Selene asked, carefully observing his reaction, yet Marek didn't seem to be in the least bit surprised.

"I'd say that was incredibly irresponsible. Do you have any idea what you've done?" Marek asked.

"No! Of course I don't, because you haven't told me what's going on! It's just one inexplicable occurrence after another in this place, and you didn't even bat an eyelid when I told you I can do magic!" Selene yelled, losing her cool.

Marek groaned aloud as he pulled the jeep around to the front of the house. "Selene, this place, well, things happen here. I knew when you and your friends arrived that it wasn't by coincidence—just like I knew you would have supernatural abilities. I just didn't know what, or if you were even aware of them yet."

"What? How?" Selene gasped.

"Because I have powers too." Marek sighed, leaning his head against the headrest.

Selene smiled, in spite of herself. "Really? Like what?"

Marek turned and looked at her so intently she felt herself blush. "Well, I have super human strength, and

I don't have to physically touch something to inflict it and I can also talk to animals—both of which you witnessed earlier. I also have an affiliation for plants and nature and can use either their elements or tap into their source to control them."

"I knew you were talking to that cat!" Selene stated gleefully.

"Not the point." Marek stated.

"Then what is?" Selene asked.

Marek reached out and grabbed her hand, and it was all she could do to concentrate on what he was saying, rather than the way her hand tingled at his touch.

"You exposed yourself when you used your powers in the pub. Did you not see the guy in the booth?"

Selene nodded slowly. "I did—he looked like he was passed out, huddled in the corner."

"Number one rule in Auberon—things are rarely as they seem. He was there waiting for you. Watching you. He was also at the pub the night you and your friends arrived and has been lurking ever since, waiting for confirmation that you are who we all think you are."

"And who do you think we are?" Selene asked quietly.

"The Auberon Witches. Returned."

Chapter Six

Cassie

Standing on her tiptoes, Cassie ran her fingers over the lock and felt a tingling sensation run through her fingertips, almost like a light electrical charge. She turned and scanned the room, trying to see something she could stand on for a better view. Her eyes fell on the squat, round velvet pouf and decided to give it a shot. She pushed it over to the bookcase and stepped up onto it, giving herself a perfectly unobstructed view of the lock. Cassie felt an energy surrounding her, drawing her to the lock as though they were both magnets. All other thoughts faded away and the only thing Cassie could focus on was the lock—and how to open it. She stared at it, willing it to open by the power of her telekinesis, but all she did was give herself a headache. With a cranky sigh, Cassie reached down and picked the book up from where it rested on the next shelf and replaced it over the lock, adding 'find the key' to her to-do-list. It was only then that she noticed the title, etched on the spine in gold cursive.

The Sisterhood

The sound of someone clearing their throat behind her startled Cassie, and in her haste to turn around, she slipped off the pouf and fell. Powerful arms caught her, and Cassie yelped as she quickly pulled away from the intruder.

"You!" she exclaimed angrily. "What the hell are you doing sneaking up on me? Better yet, what the hell are you doing here full stop? You might be the landlord, but you have no right to just walk in here whenever you want."

Ravi just chuckled, unaffected by Cassie's anger. "The front door was wide open. I called out but when I didn't get any answer, I had reason to be concerned there could be someone in here ransacking the place." He smirked, and Cassie's scowl deepened.

"You're full of shit! I would have heard you if you'd called out, so tell me what you're really doing here before I call the police!" Cassie yelled, her hands on her hips.

"Be my guest." He said, gesturing towards the kitchen. "I just had lunch with the sheriff and I'd be more than happy to give you his direct number." He smiled his perfect smile.

"You think you're just so charming, don't you! Well, you're not. You're just another smug, rich, white guy who thinks he can get whatever he wants and do whatever he wants." Cassie glowered at him.

"If that's the case then, Cassie, tell me what it is that you want?" he took a step towards her but she held her ground.

"I want you to get the hell out of here and leave me alone." she stated.

Ravi chuckled, and turned away before glancing back over his shoulder. "By the way, did you take a look at the base of the owl?"

Cassie looked at him, her eyebrows raised as she wondered how he could have known about it. As though amused by her surprise, he grinned and gave her a brief salute. Then he vanished.

Cassie yelped and stared at the empty space before her, her hands clamped over her mouth.

Our landlord just disappeared into nothing. That just happened.

When she felt that she could move again, Cassie walked forward, waving her hands in front of her like she would be able to still feel Ravi standing there.

How the hell did he do that?

Cassie hurried back the shelves and pulled the owl down, turning it over to inspect its base. She held it up closer as she tried to read an inscription.

To My Dear Cassiopeia, Happy Anniversary. With all my love until the end of time, Ravi.

All Cassie could do was stare at it, reading the words but not understanding them

What the f…

As the front door slammed, Cassie jumped and walked towards the foyer just in time to see Selene throw the front door open and storm in, her expression thunderous.

"So, the date went well?" Cassie joked, but Selene remained silent as she continued into the kitchen.

"Uh, did something happen?" she asked Marek as he appeared in the doorway.

"You could say that. Has anything happened here? Anything out of the ordinary?" he asked, stopping at the doorway as he peered in after Selene, but she was out of sight.

"Out of the ordinary?" It was all Cassie could do not to laugh. Everything they'd experienced since arriving in Auberon was out of the ordinary. "Like what?"

Marek shrugged. "Just anything that seemed strange…"

"Well if you call the landlord rocking up before disappearing into thin air strange…" Cassie tried to make it sound like she was joking as she gauged his reaction.

"Ravi was here? How long ago?" Marek asked.

"He left right before you arrived." Cassie said, her laughter falling away as she saw the serious expression of Marek's face.

"Anything else?" he asked, but Cassie shook her head, not wanting to say any more until they had Addie back.

"Do you mind if I come in for a bit?" he asked.

"Only if you tell me what's going on." Cassie agreed as she stepped aside.

Marek nodded again and strode into the foyer. "Can you get Selene? I don't think I'm her favourite person at the moment, but it's important I speak to you both."

"Uh, okay. I'd say she's probably in the kitchen. Let's just go in there." Cassie led the way, but as she walked into the kitchen, she saw Selene standing at the windows, looking out into the garden.

"Hey, Selene, Marek needs to talk to us." Cassie said quietly, taking a seat at the kitchen island while Marek leaned against the door frame.

"Selene?" Cassie prompted, when her friend didn't turn around.

"There is a really big dog outside. Actually, it looks more like a wolf." Selene replied without turning around and Cassie jumped off the stool and hurried over for a closer look.

Outside, in the middle of the garden, sat the largest dog Cassie had ever seen.

Or is it a wolf?

Its shoulders were broad for an animal, and its paws looked like they were as big as her own hands. Its fur was grey, darker on the ears and along the nose, but it also seemed to have a purple tinge to it along its chest. Cassie heard Marek walk up behind them, before he went to the door and stepped outside.

"Wait! It might be dangerous!" Selene cried, but he ignored them.

As he approached the animal, it raised its paw up to Marek, who extended his hand and shook it.

"Are you seeing this?" Cassie asked Selene.

"I don't know what I'm seeing anymore." Selene replied, not taking her eyes off the animal and Marek, her hand pressed to the glass.

As they watched on, Marek stepped aside, and the animal's paw returned to the ground as the pair of them looked up at the manor.

"What are they looking at?" Selene asked.

"I have no idea. But I want to find out." Cassie stepped back from the window.

"Wait for me!" Selene said and followed her.

Cassie led them out to Marek and the animal who didn't move a muscle as they approached. Cassie stood next to them and looked up at the house, Selene beside her.

"Uh, what are we looking at?" Selene whispered to her and Cassie was about to tell her that she didn't know, when she noticed a slight glimmer to a section of the wall on the second floor. She raised her hand up to point it out to Selene.

"What is that?" Selene asked.

"Yeah, Marek, what is that?" Cassie turned to him but he didn't answer.

Suddenly the house seemed to shudder and shake, as though there was an earthquake, yet the ground was stable where they stood.

"Something's happening inside!" Cassie declared as she ran back in.

"Wait! Is that a good idea?" Selene yelled after her, but Cassie didn't care. She just wanted answers.

A roar sounded through the house, as loud as a train running through the subway—and it seemed to originate from the floor above them. Cassie ran towards the stairs and took them two at a time. As her feet hit the landing, there came a flash of brilliant purple light from the middle of the hallway. She threw her arm up over her eyes to protect them from the flash, only lowering it again once it subsided.

"What the… *Addie*?!"

Destiny Revealed

Chapter One

Addie

L ooking around frantically, trying to get her bearings, the screams she left behind still echoing in her ears. Addie forced herself to breathe, taking in the cream ceiling above her and the wooden floor beneath leading over to the banister at the top of the staircase and she realized she was sprawled across the landing of the second floor of the manor. Her head was pounding and she clasped her hand against it as she slowly sat up.

Please let this be 2020 again.

At the sound of someone running up the stairs, Addie tried to stand up, but her ankle throbbed as fiercely as her head, and she winced trying to put weight on it. Instead, using her hands and her good foot, she scooted backwards as quickly as she could. Thoughts of the warlock coming after her and doing to her whatever he'd done to the other Addie made her feel sick to her stomach as she imagined him coming up the stairs to get her.

No, no, no. I did not just go through all of that just to be killed by the warlock anyway.

Addie glanced behind her, looking for somewhere to hide. Seeing a door, she shoved herself over to the wall as the footsteps grew louder. Her panic threatened to take a hold as she struggled to reach the doorknob, her fingers just brushing the edge of it.

"Addie?"

Addie turned around, her mouth falling open she saw Cassie standing at the top of the stairs looking just as surprised as Addie felt.

"Cassie! Is that really you? The now you?" Addie asked.

"Uh…I don't know what you mean by the 'now you' but yeah, it's me. Are you okay? We've been worried sick." Cassie said as she hurried over and helped her friend to her feet.

Addie braced herself against the wall and Cassie's shoulder as she gingerly touched her sore foot to the floor. "I'm okay. I think I just landed on my foot the wrong way."

"Landed the wrong way? What are you talking about? Where have you been?" Cassie asked, her voice full of concern.

"I'll explain everything, but please just help me get downstairs first. I can't be on the landing. He killed Addie, and he'll kill me next." Addie sobbed, her fear subsiding to relief at her return to the right time and place.

"Addie, you're not making any sense. No one's killed you, you're perfectly fine." Cassie tried to reassure her. "I mean, you look and smell like you could use a bath and probably a stiff drink too, but aside from that…"

"Wow, I forgot how tactful you are." Addie said dryly, grimacing as she tried her best to hobble alongside Cassie. Before Cassie could reply, a dog's bark sounded up the stairs.

"I'm gone five minutes and you get a dog?" Addie asked.

"We didn't. It literally showed up in the back yard right before you reappeared." Cassie explained.

"You know what, I don't think anything can surprise me anymore." Addie said.

"Yeah, me either." Cassie admitted as the dog reached the landing and barked loudly in greeting.

As soon as Addie saw the dog, looking up at her with its deep blue eyes, she knew it was Jove. "It's you! But how?" Without thinking, she stepped forward on her sore foot and yelped in pain. The dog shuddered, growling deep and low and within a matter of seconds the dog was gone and Jove was in its place, crouching on the floor.

"I take it back. I'm surprised." Cassie squeaked.

Jove stood and a smile spread across his face as he stared at Addie, his black hair as scruffy as the thin beard which lined his jaw.

Oh my, he's even more handsome than I remember.

"Oh! He's naked!" Cassie yelped, turning her head before quickly turning back again. "Yep. He's definitely naked!" She clasped her free hand over her eyes, though it didn't hide the grin on her face.

Jove didn't seem to notice as he walked towards Addie, his hand held out to her. "I'm so relieved you made it back safely. I was so worried when I followed you out of the cavern and you weren't here."

Addie removed her hand from where it was pressed against the wall and placed it in his. "You followed me? I don't know what happened, but I went back in time."

Jove's eyes widened. "That's most unusual. We need to tell the others." Without another word, Jove scooped her up in his arms and turned to Cassie. "After you."

"Uh…" Was all Cassie said as she looked from Jove to Addie and then walked to the stairs, taking them two at a time.

Addie wrapped her arms around Jove's neck and when he turned to look at her, their faces were so close she knew if she wanted to, she could kiss him again.

"Are you sure you're okay?" Jove whispered.

"I am now." Addie replied. She watched as his stare moved to her mouth, and her heart quickened with the anticipation of repeating the magical kiss they'd shared in the cavern.

"Are you guys coming, or what?" Cassie called up from the bottom of the stairs, ruining the moment.

"I'm sorry, Cassie has impeccable timing." Addie explained.

Jove grinned. "We have plenty of time to get acquainted." With the smile still in place, he carried Addie down the stairs to where Cassie was waiting.

"Oh, shit, bloody hell!" Cassie screeched as she saw them and covered her hand over her eyes again.

Addie giggled to herself.

It's good to be back.

Chapter Two

Selene

The shimmering against the side of the house grew brighter, and as Selene stood on the grass with Marek, a large circular window appeared. The shimmering subsided and three figures appeared within the frame. Selene frowned, raising her hand to shield her eyes as she tried to get a better look. She gasped as she saw three women standing there, staring down at them.

"Marek, look! They look exactly like us!" Selene exclaimed in a hushed whisper. Marek didn't answer but reached out and grabbed her free hand and gave it a gentle squeeze.

"Look out, naked man approaching!" Cassie declared loudly as she strode through the back door towards them.

"What are you..." Selene started to ask, but the question fell away as Jove followed, Addie in his arms. "Addie! You're back!" Releasing Marek's hand, Selene hurried over and awkwardly threw her arms around Addie. "I'm so glad you're okay."

"Oh, she's great. Ask her why a naked stranger just carried her through the house—you're going to love this, Selene." Cassie stated with a cheeky grin, keeping her back to Jove.

"Uh, that's actually an interesting point. Who are you and where did you come from?" Selene asked.

"It's complicated…" Jove started, gently, lowering Addie to the ground, but keeping his arm firmly around her waist.

"Okay…care to elaborate on that? And while you're at it, why do you two look so cosy?" Selene frowned. "Am I missing something? Am I the only one confused?"

"Nope. Right there with you." Cassie agreed. "But before we talk about anything, can we please get this man some clothes? It's distracting."

Jove grinned, and Marek chuckled. "I usually have spare clothes floating around in the jeep. I'll be right back."

"In the meantime, how about we go back inside?" Cassie said as she turned and walked back towards the house, her hand still over her eyes.

Chapter Three

Cassie

As they settled in the kitchen, Marek appeared with a pair of jeans and a red flannel shirt. "Sorry, that's all I could find."

"Thanks, Marek. It will do me until I get home." Jove replied, making sure Addie was comfortable on the stool before he proceeded to get dressed there and then.

"Wait—you two know each other?" Selene asked, looking from Marek to Jove and back again.

"We've been friends a long time." Marek said.

"Okay," Selene rubbed her forehead. "But do all your friends come to visit naked?"

Marek burst out laughing while Jove looked sheepish. "You know that huge dog we saw outside?"

Selene nodded, wondering what one thing had to do with the other.

"Well, meet Jove." Marek gestured towards his friend.

"Ruff!" Jove said as he bowed.

Marek walked over and casually draped his arm over her shoulder. "Jove is a shifter. You first saw him as a dog, and now you can see him in his human form." Marek exclaimed.

"What? Werewolves are real?" Selene asked, her eyes wide.

"No. They're not. I'm not a werewolf—I'm a shifter, which means I can turn into any creature I want. I just prefer to be a dog." Jove explained, taking the stool beside Addie.

Selene nodded slowly, looking pointedly at Cassie.

"Believe me, I'm just as surprised as you. But I saw it with my own eyes. He came upstairs as a dog and then changed." Cassie explained.

Selene walked over to the fridge without a word and pulled out a bottle of water. By the time she'd turned around and placed it on the kitchen island, it was an icy cold bottle of sauvignon blanc.

"Are you okay?" Addie asked her.

With a sigh, Selene began pouring them each a glass. "I suppose so. I just have so many questions."

"Don't we all." Cassie said dryly as she reached for a glass and took a large sip. "First of all, give me a look at that ankle." She gestured for Addie to lift her foot up on the empty stool beside her, where she started running her hand over it as she continued. "Secondly, I want to know why you two keep looking all doe-eyed at each other. It's weird."

"I don't know what to say," Addie started, looking at Jove as he reached across the bench and grabbed her hand. "He saved my life."

"He saved your life? From who? What?" Cassie cut in.

"I'll get to that in a minute." Addie playfully swiped at Cassie. "Trust me, I know it must seem crazy—I would think it was crazy if I was on the outside looking in, but as soon as I saw Jove, there was an instant connection. It was as though I'd known him forever, like we were two kindred spirits seeing each other for the first time in ages. There's just such a strong pull whenever we're near each other. I don't know how to explain it…"

"Well, I don't believe in love at first site, but whatever." Cassie said dismissively, annoyed with herself for feeling jealous and not wanting the others to see it in her expression and she removed her hands from Addie's ankle.

"What? That actually feels better." Addie said, running her hand over it while grinning up at Cassie. "I love this having power gig."

"You're welcome. Now, what I want to know, is where have you been? What happened? How did your knight in shining armour save you?" Cassie asked, returning to her glass of wine.

Addie took a deep breath and filled them in on her misadventures, and Cassie heard the tremor in her friend's voice as she described the warlock crashing the party and the demise of the other Addie.

"I know we've seen them in the photographs," Cassie said from where she leaned against the counter, "But what was it like to actually be in the same room as one of them?"

"It was the strangest thing I've ever experienced." Addie confirmed.

"You mean stranger than instantly falling in love with a shifter you met in a cavern?" Cassie stated dryly and Addie rolled her eyes.

"The room was so strange. It was in the manor, but it didn't look like any of the rooms we went through." Addie said.

"It's probably just been redecorated. That was 1920, after all?" Selene suggested.

Addie shook her head. "No, I don't think so. It had a massive circular window, and we definitely don't have those here."

Cassie straightened. "I saw something like that in some of the photographs! I checked the manor from the outside I couldn't see it anywhere."

"We saw it." Selene said quietly.

"What do you mean?" Addie asked as she and Cassie stared over at her.

"Cassie, remember when we were outside, just before Addie came back, and there was that strange noise coming from the manor and the wall outside looked strange? Like it was shimmering or something?" Selene asked.

Cassie nodded. "Though I'm not convinced it wasn't anything more than a trick of the light."

Selene shook her head. "You're such a sceptic, Cassie. It wasn't. After you ran inside, the shimmering increased, and the circle window revealed itself."

"How do you mean it revealed itself?" Cassie asked.

"Exactly that. One minute it wasn't there and then the next, it wasn't. That's not all though. Standing at the window, looking out at us, were the three women. You know, us, but not." Selene explained with a confident enthusiasm.

"Were they dressed in old-fashioned clothes? Like from the twenties?" Addie asked.

Selene shook her head. "There were dressed in old fashioned clothes, yes, but older than the 1920s. It was hard to see too clearly, but they looked as though they were wearing black dresses with high collars and long sleeves and white bonnets. They were only there for a moment, and then the window disappeared."

"My guess is it appeared while Addie was trying to return to the manor," Marek said, "And then disappeared once she was safely back."

"Like the portal I came through let them reveal the room, but once the portal closed again it was gone?" Cassie replied.

Marek shrugged. "It's just a theory, but the timing of both can't be coincidental."

"I think we have a bigger problem we need to deal with first." Selene stated, tapping the empty bottle of wine three times and magically refilling it.

"Have I told you you're my new best friend?" Cassie grinned and slid her empty glass towards Selene.

"Not today. Anyway, I want to know more about this warlock." Selene replied.

Addie shuddered. "He was awful—and so strong, like crazy strong. And angry. So full of hatred, I could see it in his eyes as he came at me. I honestly believe he would have killed me if Jove hadn't shown up."

"Are we safe from him now, though? Here? How do we know he hasn't followed you through the last portal?" Selene asked.

"Honestly, I'm not one hundred percent certain, but as I jumped through the portal, I imagined it sealing up behind me, leaving nothing but a brick wall and a dead end." Addie explained.

"Is it really that simple?" Cassie asked, not looking convinced.

"I think so. I mean, I'm still not exactly sure how I do it at all, but I think if he'd followed me, we'd know about it by now." Addie said.

"Was it really him?" Marek asked Jove, who nodded in reply. Marek swore under his breath.

"Okay, you guys can't keep doing this. It's annoying." Selene said crankily.

"What's annoying?" Marek asked, his eyes wide.

"You keep secrets! You tell us what you think we need to know and withhold everything else and it's not fair! We deserve to know what's going on." Selene folded her arms across her chest and scowled.

Marek sighed and pulled Selene against him, wrapping his arms around her and planting a kiss on the top of her head, despite her own arms remaining folded.

Cassie made a retching noise and rolled her eyes but was ignored.

Ugh. These guys are killing me with all this lovely dovey rubbish.

"I'm sorry." Marek said to Selene. "I'm not intentionally trying to keep you uniformed, I'm just trying to protect you."

"Marek, have you ever heard the phrase, 'Knowledge is Power?" Cassie interrupted, raising her glass to him as though toasting before she winked and took a sip.

"Okay, okay. Damn it you're a feisty bunch." Marek groaned. "The Warlock you saw, his name is Brenner, and the last time he was seen in this realm was right here at the manor during a New Year's Eve party in 1920."

"Wait—that's where—when—I was?" Addie said in a hushed voice.

"Shh, let him continue." Selene hissed.

"Three women lived in the manor, cousins I think they were, if my memory serves me. Anyway, Brenner managed to kill one of them, before the other two could stop his destruction and while the cousins couldn't kill him, they were able to banish him to another dimension. It was supposed to be permanent, and no one except the remaining cousins knew where he was sent. That is, until you entered the cavern, Addie." Marek explained.

Cassie looked at Addie who looked like she was about to cry, and reached out and patted her arm.

"So it's my fault the other Addie was killed. I led the warlock straight to her." Addie whispered.

"Yes and no. It was already in the past, so it was always going to happen. You can't change the past." Jove said.

"How did you end up in the cavern in the first place?" Marek asked.

Addie looked from Selene to Cassie, her expression questioning.

"Fair's fair. No secrets from either side if we want to get to the bottom of this." Selene said, finally unfolding her arms and stepping back from Marek, but she grabbed his hand as he went to lift his arm up from her around her shoulders.

Cassie shrugged. "I agree."

"Okay. Well, basically the three of us saw a weird figure in the garden and we followed it through the woods to an old, rickety bridge that led to some old ruins. In the middle of the ruins was a giant stone urn." Cassie said matter-of-factly.

"You three saw a strange figure and just decided to follow it? Who does that?" Marek looked at them, wide-eyed.

Cassie shrugged. "It's been crazy from the moment we met each other at the airport, so I figured we should just embrace it."

"I was the first to wake up." Addie said.

"What?" Marek asked, looking at Selene, "You were unconscious?"

"Shh.." Selene shushed him.

"As I was saying," Addie continued, "I was the first to wake up. I don't really remember what happened, but we were all lying on the ground before the urn and the figure was gone."

"Except for their cloak." Cassie added.

Addie nodded. "I tried to wake Cassie and Selene up but I couldn't. Then I saw a strange colored smoke coming from the urn and I kind of just fell in while I was checking it out. It was like I was Alice in Wonderland, just falling and falling and I wondered if it would ever stop when I landed in the caves. The figure was there, watching me, and I followed it through the tunnels and into a large cavern. The rest, I've already told you."

"Do you know who the figure was?" Selene asked Marek.

He shook his head. "I've never seen anything like that, which is concerning. Though it definitely sounds like it knew who you were. Did you have your powers before your encounter with the creature?" he asked.

The women each shook their heads. "At least, not that we were aware of, or not to the extent that we have now." Cassie confirmed.

"All I can think of is that the creature was sent here somehow to lure you to the ruins to activate your powers, so that you would release Brenner."

"Well, that's shitful." Cassie scoffed.

"Would the creature have any connection to the creepy guy we saw?" Selene asked Marek.

"What creepy guy?" Addie asked.

Selene filled the others in their minor mishap in town, including the part where she performed her magic in the open.

"The Cult?" Jove asked Marek.

"I think so." Marek nodded and Jove let out a long, low whistle.

"The who?" Selene asked.

"The Cult are a group of magical hunters. They're kind of like reapers for the magic community and they hunt down powerful sources of magic and drain it from its source as a means of sustenance. They're barely cognitive and extremely dangerous." Jove explained.

"So let me see if we have this right. There's a warlock on the loose after a hundred years that wants to kill us, and a creepy cult dude that wants our magic?" Cassie stated.

"Yeah, that pretty much sums it up." Marek confirmed.

"Right. Well, what else did I miss while I was gone?" Addie asked, half-jokingly.

"Well, nothing quite as exciting as you all, but I had little adventure in the living room with an owl and the landlord." Cassie said, and proceeded to tell them about the sudden appearance of Ravi and the strange inscription at the base of the owl. As she spoke, she noticed the curious looks between Jove and Marek, and once she'd finished her explanation, Cassie demanded they explain themselves.

"All we know, is that from the moment the three of you arrived in Auberon, strange things have happened—and not just to the three of you. Ravi, Jove and I have undergone changes too." Marek explained.

"Really?" Selene asked. "Like how? Do you have powers too?"

"Well, my first shift took place after your arrival." Jove confirmed. "I knew it was always a possibility and when I first heard of your arrival I wondered if the time had come. Though it wasn't until I sensed that Addie was in trouble that it happened. And before you ask—I don't know how I knew. I just did."

"What about you?" Selene asked, looking up at Marek.

"Well, it's a bit different for me. I come from a long family line of protectors. My parents told me stories of the Auberon witches ever since I was a child. Though to be honest, I always thought it was an urban legend. Until you arrived. I was reading when I heard a phone ringing—only it wasn't the land line. I hunted through the house, trying to work out where it was coming from, and I found it on top of the bookcase, covered in dust. I was stumped—as you know Auberon doesn't get cell reception. Yet, there I was, holding a ringing phone in my hand. I answered it and a voice told me it was time to serve the order, and I was to go and meet the Auberon witches as they had returned."

"Why didn't you say anything that first night?" Selene asked.

"Well, because I didn't know how much the three of you knew about Auberon and your legacy. If I'd just blurted it out on the drive into town, would you have believed me?" Marek asked.

"No bloody way. I'm still finding it hard to believe now." Cassie laughed.

"So that's why your phone worked while we were at the pub?" Selene asked.

Marek nodded. "The order called to make sure I was with you. I suspect they already knew Brenner was free from his exile."

The group quieted, each letting the flood of information sink in. Cassie found herself thinking about Ravi, with his handsome, albeit cocky, looks and the way he always seemed to have a twinkle in his eye. It both annoyed and intrigued her. "What's Ravi's deal?" Cassie asked, playing with her wine glass while trying to pretend she wasn't interested in the answer.

"Best let Ravi tell his own story." Jove suggested.

"That's thoughtful of you, Jove." Ravi said as he suddenly appeared next to Cassie and in her surprise, she staggered and almost tripped over the stool. Ravi reached out and grabbed her by the waist to stop her, and she felt an instant rush of electricity surge through her. Looking up, she met his mischievous stare and she swallowed thickly as he grinned at her. Cassie realized everyone's eyes were on them and she squirmed out of Ravi's grasp and slapped him across the face.

"Cassie!" Selene chastised her, but Ravi just burst into laughter. Cassie scowled at the sound, and turned her back to him while her heart did little flips in her chest.

"That is so cool that you become invisible." Addie said and Cassie rolled her eyes at her friends attempt to diffuse the situation.

"I'm still getting used to it." Ravi admitted. "The first time it happened, I completely freaked out until I returned back to normal. Like the rest of you, my powers only kicked in when you arrived in town. Turns out I can also astral project and teleport."

"Okay, I'm super jealous." Addie said.

"That's all well and good, but I'm pretty sure you're not supposed to use your powers to spy on people like some supernatural peeping tom." Cassie scowled.

"I wasn't spying. I was making sure you were safe." Ravi explained.

"I can look after myself, thank you very much." Cassie snapped.

"Besides, if it wasn't for me, you would never have found the lock." Ravi said.

Cassie turned and glared at him. "That was you knocking shit off the shelf?"

Ravi grinned, clearly pleased with himself. "At the rate you were going, it would have been weeks before you found it."

"What lock?" Selene asked.

"I'll show you." Cassie said, hopping off her stool and shoving her elbow into Ravi's side as she stormed past him.

In the living room, Cassie dragged the stool back over to the bookshelf and pulled the book from the shelf before hopping back down. "It's right there, in the wall. This book looks like it might have once stored the key, but it's empty." She opened it to show them.

"Well that's perfect." Selene sighed, crossing her arms against her chest. "Another mystery we have no clue how to solve."

"Uh, guys…" Addie said, and as they all turned, she grabbed at a delicate silver chain hanging around her neck and pulled it from beneath her dress. Hanging from the end was an ornate key.

"Where did you get that from?" Cassie asked, reaching out to touch it. She felt like she'd seen it before, but she knew she hadn't.

"The other Addie gave it to me right before she went to fight Brenner." Addie explained.

"Well what are we waiting for?" Jove said, gently pushing Addie towards the stool. "See if it fits the lock." Addie stepped up onto the stool as Jove protectively placed his hands around her waist.

"It fits!" Addie cried and Cassie clapped her hands together, hoping they were about to get some answers.

"Blast…" Addie said.

"What is it?" Selene asked.

"Well, it fits, but when I turn it nothing happens." Addie said.

"Let me try." Cassie demanded, replacing Addie on the stool, but it was the same thing.

"This is so frustrating," Selene moaned. "We have a mismatched lock and key and a disappearing window. Neither of which are any help protecting us from what's after us."

"There are some family tomes back at my house that might hold the answers we need." Marek said. "If anyone had information about all this stuff, it would be the order, right?"

"It's worth a shot." Cassie agreed. "Why don't you take Selene and go and grab them?"

"I think it'best that we all stick together." Jove cut in. "We don't know if the cult will be back—or Brenner for that matter."

"I think Jove's right. After seeing that creepy… thing… in town, I'd feel much better knowing we have our combined powers if we run into them again. Especially since we're still working them out." Selene confirmed.

"Right. Well let's go." Cassie declared, leading them out of the manor, making sure to keep distance between herself and Ravi. As she watched him climb into the front passenger seat, her annoyance grew that he didn't bother to ask anyone else if they wanted the seat.

Stop it. You're being petty. You don't even want the front seat. Or is it because you want him to sit in the back with you?

Cassie scowled as she climbed into the back next to Selene. Addie was about to join them when Jove reached out and grabbed her hand. "I need to shift. Would you mind bringing my clothes along for me?" he asked. Addie grinned and the two stepped back from the car. Both Cassie and Selene leaned forward, wanting to watch. Jove stood back from the car, and closing his eyes, his whole body seemed to both shimmer and vibrate before seemed to vanish before their eyes. On hearing a small yap, they looked down at the pile of clothes on the ground to find a raggedy looking puppy instead of a brazen, wolf-life dog.

"Okay that was awesome." Selene confirmed. "He's so adorable!"

Addie scooped both Jove and his clothes up in her arms, and got into the car, placing them on her lap as she closed the door behind them.

"Can I pat him?" Selene asked as Jove ran across their laps and licked her hands. Addie and Selene giggled.

"This is just straight up bizarre. You guys realise there's a naked man there somehow, right?" Cassie made a face and tried to press herself up against the seat as Jove scurried across her lap.

"Stay alert." Marek instructed sternly as he started the car and pulled out of the driveway.

Chapter Four

Selene

The drive took them through the town and Selene shuddered as they drove past the pub as she thought back to their attacker. She felt like Addie or Cassie weren't as concerned by what was happening— that she was the only one that was scared. Her new-found friends seemed more concerned with touching or avoiding being touched by the puppy version of Jove. Selene, on the other hand, sat with her hands across her stomach, as it cramped and fluttered with nerves. She didn't think she'd ever felt so anxious in her life.

Just before they reached the outskirts of town, Marek steered the jeep off the main road and onto a narrow dirt track that weaved through the forest. Despite her fear, Selene found herself admiring the surrounding trees. They rose into the sky, with their skinny trunks and sparse branches. The sunlight filtered through the treetops causing shadows to dance across the ground. It gave the forest a hypnotic quality, and somehow made her feel a little calmer.

They pulled up in front of a large cabin, constructed by row upon row of logs that Selene imagined were the same as those surrounding the property. It was a single story, but it was sprawling, topped with narrow peaked rooves of dark slate. To Selene, it looked more like a home than the sterile mansion she'd lived in with her husband.

As they piled out of the car, Addie followed Jove as he leaped out of the car and ran around to the back of the car.

"You're not going to just stand there and watch him, are you?" Cassie asked.

"Well I can't just put his clothes on the ground! They'll get dirty!" Addie exclaimed with a grin.

"You could at least turn your back to him, you perve." Cassie retorted.

"Too late!" Addie giggled as Jove suddenly sprung up before her.

"Ugh." was Cassie's response as she walked towards the house.

"I think they're sweet together." Selene whispered as she walked beside her.

"Would that be because you're all loved up with Mr Protector over here?" Cassie asked, nodding towards Marek's back as he stepped up onto the porch to unlock the front door.

"Shh!" hissed Selene, nudging Cassie in the ribs as she watched Marek to make sure he hadn't heard.

Marek pushed the front door open and stepped aside. "Welcome to my humble home." He waited until everyone was inside before he closed and locked it behind them. "Make yourselves at home. There's not much in the fridge except a few beers, but you're welcome to anything you can find. I'll go and find these books, if you want to help me, Selene?"

She nodded, the flurry of nerves returning, only this time they had nothing to do with an impending attack and everything to do with being alone with Marek. She followed him silently through the cabin until he led her into what looked like a large study, lined on either side with floor-to-ceiling shelves overflowing with books. The rear of the room had a long, narrow window that ran the length of the wall, letting in what natural light managed to filter down through the trees. Selene hovered over a wooden coffee table in the centre of the room that was flocked on either side by worn lounge chairs. She felt awkward just standing there, but had no idea what Marek was looking for. So instead, she pretended to admire the room while she covertly watched Marek run his long fingers along the spines of the books, the muscles of his arms apparent under his shirt. Selene found herself wondering what his muscles looked like without the shirt and as though sensing her eyes on him, he spoke softly.

"I was hoping we could take this opportunity to talk." he said softly.

Selene was grateful his back was still turned, as she blushed at her interrupted thoughts.

"Uh, sure. What did you want to talk about?" she asked.

"I know the timing is shit, but it's doing my head in. The kiss…I wanted to know…"

"It was a mistake." Selene cut him off, turning away from him, fearing if he looked at her, he'd see the lie in her eyes.

Marek didn't say anything for a moment, but she could hear him pulling books from the shelves. Swallowing the lump in her throat, Selene distracted herself by reading the titles of the books piled on the table, each of them with pieces of paper sticking out from their pages, marking places. She jumped when Marek whispered over her shoulder.

"Why?"

"Why what?" Selene asked, spinning around.

"Why was it a mistake?" Marek asked, his eyes searching hers in a way that made her feel completely exposed and it made her want to run from the room.

"How many reasons do you want?" she asked, trying to make light of the situation but failing.

Marek reached out and grabbed her hand. "I know it's crazy, that we've just met, but I've seen the way you look at me and I know you feel the connection between us as strongly as I do. The whole time I was listening to Addie try to explain her connection with Jove, I knew exactly how she felt. It's how I've felt about you since the moment I saw you on the side of the road."

"Maybe there is a connection," Selene admitted, "But it doesn't change anything." She was trying her best to avoid looking at him, staring instead at her hand clasped in his. She willed herself to let go, but her hand appeared to have a life of its own.

"What could possibly negate a connection with someone?" Marek asked.

"We're just not well suited is all." Selene stammered.

"Why? Because you're rich and I'm not?" Marek asked.

"I don't care about money and if you knew me at all, you would know that." Selene said.

"Hmm, that's all well and good coming from someone that's always had it. Regardless, I want to get to know you. I want to know everything." he whispered.

"We come from two very different worlds." Selene added, trying to sound convincing.

"And yet, here you are, in mine. The world hasn't ended." Marek confirmed. "Is that the best you've got?"

"I'm also a good ten years older than you, which is ridiculous in itself…"

"What's ridiculous is using age as an excuse." Marek cut in.

"You know I'm married, right?" Selene asked, finally turning around to face him, certain that fact would stop him in his tracks.

Instead, Marek nodded. "I do. I also know you left him."

Selene felt lost for words as she stared down at her feet. Her attraction to Marek had terrified her from the moment they first met, and it only intensified with each meeting. It was like nothing she'd ever experienced before and Selene felt torn between wanting to run towards it and wanting to run from it. As though taking her momentary silence as a crack in her defence, Marek stepped closer and lifted her chin so she had no choice but to look at him.

"Look, I know we're different, but that's what makes life interesting. Selene, I know you're spoiled and a little pretentious and you can be curt and condescending. However, you're also generous and insightful, charming, considerate and sexy as hell. I don't pretend to understand anything that's going on, but I can't ignore how I feel around you. It really does seem like the only thing that makes sense anymore. So please stop looking for reasons for us not to be together." As Selene looked up to find Marek's eyes searching her own, she felt as though the room slowly vanished around them, and nothing existed except for the two of them. Staring into Marek's eyes, Selene could have sworn she was looking into her past as well as her future, and unable to hold back another second, she threw her arms around Marek's neck and kissed him deeply.

Chapter Five

Addie

Addie sat in Marek's living room on the comfortable but well-loved lounge beside Jove, while Cassie and Ravi sat opposite. Addie found entertainment in watching Cassie scowl at Ravi while simultaneously trying to press herself against the armrest and create as much of a gap between them as possible.

"…and so, my family was entrusted with the upkeep and protection of the manor and the surrounding grounds. It's been that way for generations." Ravi said. "It wasn't until a couple of years ago, when my father passed away, that I became the landlord. It was while I was cataloguing the contents to update the insurance that I discovered that owl statue and the engraving on its base. Obviously, I didn't think it was anything more than a coincidence at the time. Then you all arrived, and well, I'm thinking there's something more to it after all."

Cassie rolled her eyes and got up from the lounge. "There's not."

Pursing her lips, Addie tried to stop the grin that threatened to reveal itself while she watched Cassie pace around the room. Addie instinctively knew it was in a desperate bid to avoid Ravi, but he didn't seem to be in the least bid distressed by Cassie's cold shoulder. In fact, at least from where Addie was sitting, he seemed as amused by Cassie's antics as Addie was.

"Hey, isn't this just like the one back at the manor?" Cassie said as she stepped aside, revealing a silver pyramid sitting on a display shelf.

"I guess so, in that they're both pyramids?" Addie replied, frowning as she peered at it.

"Well, yeah, they are, but is it the same one? I don't know, there's just something about it…" Cassie picked it up and as soon as she did, there came a mechanical groan from the wall before her.

"Uh, what did you do?" Addie asked.

"I have no idea." Cassie replied as she slowly backed away from the wall until she bumped against the lounge where Ravi still sat. As they looked on, the wall itself appeared to split in two and separate, causing everything on its shelves to rattle and shake.

"Holy shit!" Cassie exclaimed as they all looked up at a hidden cabinet with row upon row of weapons. There were swords of different shapes and lengths, maces coated with assorted implements of pain, daggers, a crossbow and arrows, and some items Addie couldn't identify.

"This is unbelievable…" Cassie said as she stepped closer and reached out to run her fingers gently over a leather-wrapped hilt.

"Don't touch them!" Addie cried.

"What do you think's going to happen?" Cassie scoffed. "They're just weapons."

"Yeah, I don't know. I agree with Addie. The way things keep happening I wouldn't tempt fate." Jove said.

"Of course you do…" Cassie trailed off, more engrossed in the display before her than any logic from the others. She appeared to be so mesmerized, that she didn't notice Ravi get up from the lounge to join her.

"Do you think Marek knows about these?" she asked to no one in particular.

"Maybe. I don't know." Ravi said, touching the opposite end of the same sword Cassie inspected. "He did say his family came from a long line of protectors, so I would think so."

Addie felt an ice-cold shiver run up her spine and she looked over her shoulder towards the window, suddenly feeling like they were being watched.

"Addie? What is it?" Jove asked.

She shook her head slowly. "I don't know. Something's wrong—or is about to be." she whispered.

"Is it one of your visions?" Cassie asked, turning away from the weapons.

"I…not exactly…It's more like a feeling…" Addie tried to explain, but she felt strange, almost as though she was only half there. The sensation made her feel uneasy and she tried not to panic, instead she reached out and grabbed Jove's hand. It made her feel a little better, but her heart still quickened and her stomach plummeted as though she was on the steep decent of a rollercoaster. "Addie? You're hurting my hand." Jove said softly, and she jumped as his voice pulled her from her thoughts.

"Oh! I'm so sorry! I didn't mean…" her voice trailed off as the room darkened, like thick clouds had just passed before the sun, yet something about the darkness felt off to Addie, unnatural.

"Marek! Selene! You'd better get out here!" she called.

"Addie, what is it? You're scaring me." Cassie said, hurrying over with Ravi right behind her.

"What's happening?" Selene asked as she and Marek came running into the living room.

"I don't know." Addie said. "Something's happening outside."

Marek strode across the room and out the front door as everyone followed close behind.

Addie was the last one outside, and she was halfway across the driveway before she looked up at the sky in awe. Gone was the cloudless blue sky that had been there upon their arrival. Now the sky was filled with billowing, dark purple clouds that lit up within with flashes of lightning, one after the other. Yet there was no thunder, no lightening extending down to the ground. A wind hurtled towards them from deep within the forest, and the trees seemed to lean forward, the whispering of their leaves a warning. Addie stepped towards them, but no one noticed, they were all too engrossed with the sky.

"I've never seen the sky look like that before…" Selene whispered. "Is this like an Auberon thing?"

Marek shook his head. "I've never seen anything like this before either."

Addie felt like she couldn't breath as her chest tightened, and a wave of dizziness swept over her. She stood still, yet she also felt as though she was moving towards the trees as their branches stretched out towards her, the tiny twigs at the branches ends reached for her like fingers trying to wrap themselves around her.

"Addie? What's wrong?" Jove asked. Addie jumped, blinking rapidly as she tried to focus on him. Glancing over her shoulder at the forest, the trees had returned to normal and she frowned, certain she hadn't imagined it.

"We need to leave. Now."

Chapter Six

Selene

"Addie? What is it? What did you see?" Selene asked, not liking the tone of her friend's voice, or the frantic look in her eyes.

"We're not safe. They're coming for us. We have to go!" Addie's voice increased in pitch with each word.

"It's okay, we're leaving. Come on." Jove placed his arm around her waist and led her towards the car. It was then Selene noticed Addie was shaking from head to toe. She felt the fear cinch around her lungs like a vice, depriving her of the ability to breathe.

"Get in the jeep. I'll be right back!" Marek instructed as he turned and ran back inside. Selene watched as he turned and ran back into the house, torn between wanting to get in the car and wanting to follow him into the house, but not feeling capable of either. As she looked back towards the jeep, she froze as three hooded men appeared in the driveway.

"Cassie!" Selene cried out as she saw one of the men blocking Ravi and Cassie from the jeep. Cassie yelped as one of the hooded men reached for her, but Ravi grabbed her hand and the two of them vanished into thin air. A loud, deep growl came from the hooded man that sent a chill of terror down Selene's spine. She felt completely paralysed, not knowing where to run or what to do.

"Marek!" she yelled, her voice a high-pitched screech as she watched the three figures turn their attention to Jove and Addie as they reached the other side of the jeep. Jove yanked the door open and shoved Addie inside before closing it again against her protests. The three cloaked figures crouched in unison, raising their arms up as Jove looked from one to the other. A low hum seemed to come from them, so low that it vibrated across the ground and up into Selene's feet. Her heart pounded against her chest and her shaky breath caught in her throat as large, fiery balls formed between their outstretched hands. Together they raised them high into the air and aimed them at Jove.

"Stop!" Selene screamed as they hurled the fiery orbs towards him, but Jove thrust his own arms out with a mighty yell and stopped the orbs in their tracks. As

Selene looked at Jove, her mouth agape, she saw the stunned expression on his face and realized he was as surprised by his feat as she was. As though Jove's new display of power instilled her with new-found confidence, Selene stepped forward and was so relieved she could move that she initially didn't realize the cloaked figures were as still as statues.

"Selene! Hurry! Get in the car! I don't know how long this will last." Jove opened the door and climbed in next to Addie.

Selene took a couple of steps forward but stopped and turned back to the house. Before she could call out to Marek once again, he came flying out the front door, three large books in his arms. "Woah!" he skidded to a stop, dropping one of the books as he saw the cloaked figures.

"It's okay!" Selene ducked down and picked up the heavy book. "Jove froze them."

"Yeah, well it looks like it's wearing off." Marek declared and as Selene stood up, she saw he was right. The cloaked figures started moving in extreme slow motion—and so too, did the fiery balls still hovering mid-air.

"Hurry!" Marek demanded, and this time Selene had no hesitation as she ran to the front passenger side of the car and got in, as Marek threw the books into the back with Addie and Jove before diving into the driver's seat. "Where's Ravi and Cassie?" he asked.

"They've already gone—I'll explain later!" Selene said, pulling on her seat belt and clutching the book to her chest.

"Oh, shit!" Jove exclaimed from the back as the cloaked figure's movements were reaching normal pace. "Go, go, go!"

Marek started the jeep and Selene braced herself as he pushed the pedal all the way to the floor, sending the car skidding across the driveway as the cloaked figures closed in.

"Marek!" Selene screeched as one of them reached for her side of the car, and she saw the festering, chalk-white of its skin and the blistering redness of its snarling mouth. Marek swore as he swerved the jeep with one hand and with the other, he thrust his arm towards the figure, sending it flying across the ground. Marek did the same to the remaining two figures, clearing the way for them to escape. Selene looked in the rear-view mirror, as they sped away, but all she could see was the dust they left in their wake.

Chapter Seven

Cassie

Cassie gasped as a cloaked figure suddenly appeared before them. The hood of the cloak hid the top of their head in shadows, but the little she could see of the creature was enough to terrify her. It opened its mouth, revealing blackened teeth and blood-tinged drool and she yelped as it lunged towards them. She felt herself yanked backwards as Ravi grabbed her by the hand, and then suddenly, the cloaked figure was gone. There was a brief sensation of weightlessness, like she was floating in the air as light as a feather, they only thing tethering her was Ravi's hand clasping her own. She tried to shake him off, wanting to see how high she could float, but he held on firmly. Then almost as quickly as it had started, the floating feeling vanished, leaving Cassie feeling as heavy as a stone. She could feel herself falling faster and faster and Cassie reached out for something to slow her decent but there was nothing.

Feeling herself slip from Ravi's grasp, she fell with a heavy bang onto the floor, hitting her head in the process. She sat up, groaning as she gingerly touched the side of her head and pulled her fingers back to find them sticky with blood.

"Cassie! Are you alright?" Ravi cried, suddenly appearing at her side.

"Huh? What…what happened? Where are we?" she asked, feeling dazed. Cassie closed her eyes, trying to remember.

"We were at Marek's," he explained as he examined the cut on her head, before rapidly unbuttoning his shirt and shrugging it off, "when members of the cult showed up. I don't know how they found us so quickly. I saw we wouldn't be able to make it to the car, so I grabbed you and teleported us out of there."

Cassie grimaced as he pressed the shirt against the side of her head. "How bad is it?"

"I'm not sure. It's hard to tell with head injuries, they always bleed terribly. Do you think you can get up off the floor if I help you?" Ravi asked.

Cassie nodded, instantly regretting as the motion increased the pain in her head, and she feared she was going to vomit all over him.

Ravi got to his feet. "Hold that shirt as tightly to your head as you can." He instructed, placing his hands under her arms and lifting her to her feet with what felt like little effort at all. He steadied her as she swayed, before leading her over to the daybed and Cassie realized they were back in the living room of the manor.

"How did we get here? What did I hit my head on? Why is it so dark?" Cassie asked, closing her eyes against the nausea as Ravi helped her to get comfortable.

"I told you—we teleported here from Marek's. I think you hit your head on the corner of that wooden box on the floor—the one with all the photograph's in it. And it's dark, because the sky is now filled with storm clouds. Only I don't think they are storm clouds."

Cassie tried to process his words, oblivious to the fact he was now sitting on the floor beside where she lay, their faces so close. "Where are the others? Did they teleport too?" she finally asked once she was able to pin down a thought.

"No. It was just you and I." Ravi said quietly.

"What? Why? We have to go back! We can't just leave them there! Those things…those *monsters*…what if they kill them? They'll all die and we just left them!" Cassie could hear herself becoming hysterical, but couldn't stop it as she tried to sit up. Ravi gently reached up and pushed her shoulders down. "You're not going anywhere until we stop that bleeding. I didn't mean to leave them. It was just a gut-reaction. All I could see was that you were in danger and that I had to get you out of there." Ravi explained.

"You have to go back for them. You have to." Cassie pleaded, reaching out for him with her free hand.

"I can't. I'm sorry, but I can't leave you here like this. Unprotected." Ravi confirmed.

Cassie let her head fall back against the cushion, unsure of whether she wanted him to stay with her, or whether she just didn't have the energy within her to argue with him to go. Instead they both sat quietly for a moment and as Ravi stroked the top of her hand with his thumb, Cassie thought how nice it was. It was such a simple gesture, the softest of touches, yet it warmed her from within. She didn't think she'd ever feel it again, not after her husband died. Opening her eyes, she carefully rolled her head to the side, keeping the shirt pressed to the other, and found Ravi staring at her intently.

"I'm scared for them." she whispered.

Ravi nodded. "Me too."

"Were they the cult members?" Cassie asked, swallowing thickly as she recalled the hideous face of the cloaked figure that had lunged at her.

"Yes." Was all Ravi said.

"Oh no, and we just left the others there. What if they couldn't get to the jeep either?" Cassie gasped.

"I'm sorry…"

"I'm not blaming you, Ravi. I'm just so scared they won't be able to get away. I don't know what I'd do without them." Cassie felt the tears trickle down her cheeks. Ravi reached up and gently wiped them away.

"They're going to be okay. The four of them are incredibly powerful, and together they'll get out of there. You just have to believe in them." Ravi whispered.

"I do. I finally believe in it all." Cassie declared, and Ravi squeezed her hand. "And Ravi? Thank you for saving me." Ravi didn't answer. Instead, he leaned forward and brushed his lips gently over Cassie's. Instantly, she felt a jolt rush through her, all the way down to her toes. Ravi pulled back slightly, and Cassie knew he was unsure of himself—something she didn't think she'd ever see. It endeared him to her even more, and she weaved her hand around the back of his neck and pulled him down towards her. As their lips met again, with a little more force this time, Cassie felt as though something hidden was unlocking inside her. In that moment, she understood exactly what Addie and Selene had been trying to explain all along. Letting Ravi in felt like going home after a long journey lost in the darkness. As their kiss deepened, Cassie felt empowered as though he completed the missing piece of herself, and she, him. Even the pain in her head subsided as she lost herself in their kiss, feeling as though they'd always been together and always would be.

Cassie pushed him away slightly, ending their kiss, and he looked at her, his eyes questioning. Smiling at him, she gave a slight nod. "I remember. I remember everything.

Destiny Forever

Chapter One

Selene

As Marek sped them along the quiet streets of Auberon, Selene flicked glances at him, her concern growing with each one. She noted the way he clenched his jaw and the protruding vein creeping along his temple. There was also the way his knuckles had turned white from gripping the steering wheel so hard. He never took his eyes off the road, and yet Selene got the impression from his unblinking stare that his mind was elsewhere. Swallowing the lump in her throat, Selene turned and looked out the rear-view mirror.

"Uh, have you guys looked back there?" she asked, her voice a little high-pitched. She didn't take her eyes off the mirror, but she could tell from Marek's swearing and the exclamations from Addie and Jove in the back seat that they could see the same ominous clouds she was looking at. The dark purple clouds appeared to be following them from where they'd left them at Marek's house, billowing angrily across the sky like a ferocious avalanche hurtling towards them.

"If I didn't know any better, I'd think those clouds were following us." Addie said from the back.

"That's because they are," Marek stated, taking a bend at such a speed that the car tilted to one side.

"Marek, maybe we should slow down, just a bit?" Selene asked, softly placing her hand on Marek's arm.

"Are you not seeing the same thing back there as the rest of us?" he replied, not looking at her.

"You're scaring me," Selene exclaimed.

"You have good reason to feel scared. We all do." Marek's admission came with a wave of anxiety so intense that Selene felt as though she was falling through the bottom of the car. As though sensing—or sharing— her increased panic, Addie reached over from the back seat and gripped her shoulder. Selene reached up and patted Addie's hand with her own, feeling comforted by the gesture.

Get it together. You need to be stronger than this. You wanted to venture out into the world on your own, so stop acting like a child.

"How much further until we reach the manor?" she asked.

"Maybe another 15, 20 minutes. I'm driving us in random circles and working us towards the manor. I'm hoping it will make it harder for anyone to follow."

Selene said nothing, but clutched the book against her chest as though it would somehow comfort her. Looking down at it, she slowly pulled it away from her chest.

"Do you guys have those other books in the back?" Selene called out.

"Yeah!" Addie replied.

"We've got about 15 minutes to get a head start on some research, don't you think?" she asked, lowering the book to her lap and opening it. Doing something other than staring at the stressed-out Marek, or at the hellish clouds behind them, made her feel a little better, and Selene threw herself into reading. The distraction worked, and she found herself engrossed in what appeared to be a hand-written history of the Auberon witches.

"Listen to this." Selene said, "This looks to be a journal or personal account. Maybe from one of the protectors? Anyway, it says here that the Auberon witches are timeless. That they appear again and again, though it's unknown how. Sometimes they are related, sisters or cousins, and other times they aren't. Regardless, they always come together to live out their destiny within each age."

"Wow. I can't even get my head around that," Addie said. "Yet, we know it must be true. I saw another version of Addie with my own two eyes. I spoke to her."

"It mentions that here too," Selene said as she read aloud another passage. "After the warlock Brenner murdered Adamina Naya in 1920, her body was not recovered and entombed as was the custom. Therefore, it was believed that the destiny of the Auberon witches was at an end."

"Well, if that was the case, how are we here, now?" Addie asked.

"I have no idea," Selene admitted. "Like everything else, we seem to discover something new, only to add a dozen more questions to the list."

"Holy shit!" Addie yelped.

"What? What is it?" Marek glanced anxiously at her through the review-mirror.

"Oh! Nothing to do with anything after us, sorry, Marek," she replied quickly.

Marek swore under his breath and Selene gave his arm a quick squeeze before she wriggled around in her seat so she could see Addie and Jove in the back. "What is it?"

Addie raised the book she had opened in her lap and turned it around so Selene could see.

"Is that... no way...!" she exclaimed.

"Can you lot tell me what all the excitement is about?" Marek called over his shoulder.

"In this book is an old photograph of a man that looks exactly like Sir Duke Dillinger." Selene explained.

"Who's he?" Marek asked, taking another corner too fast, causing everyone to brace themselves.

"He was the gentleman who offered the three of us a seat on his jet that ultimately ended up landing here," Addie explained.

"Then he left, supposedly to return, but we haven't heard from him since," Selene confirmed. "What does it say about him?"

"Well, for starters, according to this book his name is Larkin Frey, a powerful conjurer," Addie read.

"So, what? He's a witch too?" Jove asked.

"No…" Addie intoned, skimming over the page. "I don't think so—or at least, not exactly. It says here that his desire for immortality led him to commit acts against the natural order."

"What does that even mean?" Selene asked.

"It means he broke the rules," Jove explained. "Used his magic or his powers to harm and manipulate."

"The conjurer became polluted by his actions, but he still refused to give up his drive for immortality, turning him into something no longer human." Addie paused as she turned the page and gasped, spinning the book around again for Selene.

"It's the creature!" she exclaimed. "The one that led us to the ruins!"

"I can't believe this!" Addie shook her head and turned the book back around so she could continue reading. "So it's only because of his powers as a conjurer that he can make himself look human, but this creature is how he looks without it."

"Larkin was behind it all. He found us at the airport and brought us here, and then in his monstrous form, he lured us to the ruins where he knew it would trigger our powers." Selene said, her mind buzzing.

"And he lured me into the caverns, releasing Brenner," Addie mumbled. "We've been nothing more than puppets since the beginning."

"But why? How does releasing Brenner help him? Is it that he wants us dead and he thinks Brenner can do it?" Selene asked.

"Again, it looks like we have more questions than answers…" Addie said.

"… and added another enemy to the list." Selene added, reaching out and grabbing her friend's hand.

Chapter Two

Cassie

W hat do you mean, you remember everything?" Ravi asked. "Are you sure you're okay?" He inquired, reaching up to touch her head gently.

"I'm fine—better than fine." She sat up slowly, pleased to find her throbbing head didn't put up too much of a protest. "It's not the head injury either. I'm not sure how to explain it, but it's like everything has just opened up to me. I can see you and me. The others too. Here and now, but also together in the past. They're like memories, but I know that they can't be my own…" Cassie tried to stand too suddenly and a wave of dizziness almost bowled her over.

"Take it easy!" Ravi jumped to his feet to steady her. "Don't underestimate that bump on the head." He held her by the shoulders, and Cassie looked up at him with a slight smile. She raised her hand and ran her thumb over his bottom lip, before stroking his cheek.

"What is it?" Ravi asked, his eyes searching hers. "I mean, I'm not complaining about your change of heart, but it hasn't been that long since you convinced yourself that you hated me."

Cassie nodded. "That's because you're smug and annoying."

Ravi burst out laughing as Cassie grinned up at him. "Yes, I am both those things, and more. Though I'm glad you've suddenly managed to see beyond them."

"I told you—I remember everything," she replied. "Here, maybe I can show you." She placed her hands over Ravi's temples and closed her eyes, focusing on trying to share with him the memories that had returned to her. Ravi gasped, and Cassie knew it was working. He pulled her hands away, and she opened her eyes, surprised to find as she looked up at him, tears filled his eyes.

"I don't know what to say..." he whispered.

"You don't need to say anything. Just kiss me." Cassie wrapped her arms around his neck and Ravi pulled her against him as they became locked in an intense kiss. An image of her husband and her children flashed before her, and Cassie pushed herself away from him. She turned and walked away, one hand on her hip and the other over her mouth.

"Cassie? What is it?" Ravi asked.

She shook her head, feeling too overwhelmed by her emotions to speak.

If Ravi and I are each other's destinies, then what of my husband, Harley? I loved—love—him with my entire being. Our life together with our children, Shep and Olive was my entire world. So what does this mean for them?

Cassie lowered her hand from her mouth and clutched at her stomach, feeling sick with the sudden guilt.

"Cassie…" Ravi asked, gently placing his hands on her shoulders. She jumped at their sudden proximity.

She spun around, quickly wiping the tears from her eyes. "I'm sorry. I… it's just…" Cassie struggled to catch her breath.

"Hey, it's all right. Just breathe for me. When you're ready, you can tell me," Ravi said gently and pulled her against his chest. Cassie closed her eyes and focused on her breathing, forcing herself to calm down. When her thoughts settled, she stepped back and looked up at him.

"I was married. Eleven years. They were the happiest eleven years of my life. I had a family, and they were my everything. Then about a year ago, all three of them died in a hit and run. In one instant, they were taken from me," she explained tearfully.

"Oh, Cassie. I am so sorry. I don't even know what to say," Ravi whispered.

"You don't need to say anything. It's just... when those memories of who I really am returned, it felt like... like..."

"Coming home?" Ravi finished for her.

Cassie nodded as the tears started flowing again.

"And you think that by remembering us, it somehow lessens the love you have for your family?" he asked.

"Yes..." Cassie sobbed.

"Hey... it's okay, come here." He led her back to the lounge and sat her down before sitting beside her and taking both of her hands in his. "I don't know how this all works, our pasts and the present. But I know it has no impact on the love you have for your family. I promise you, our connection, our destiny or whatever you want to call it, doesn't detract from that. All right?" Ravi explained.

Cassie nodded, finding comfort in his words. Before she could say anything further, there was a knock at the front door. "I wonder who that is?" She got up from the lounge and walked out into the foyer towards the front door. As the knock came a second time, Cassie opened the door and gasped.

"Mr... I mean Sir Dillinger! What are you doing here? We thought we wouldn't see you again." Cassie stated.

He bowed his head. "Yes, I truly apologize. I'd intended to return with the plane right away, but there were complications at the other end that prevented me from returning sooner. I tried calling each of the mobile numbers you gave me, but I couldn't get through to any of them."

"Yes, apparently Auberon doesn't have cell reception," Cassie explained apologetically as she stepped aside. "Please, come in."

"Thank you," Dirk said and entered the foyer. "I didn't even know if you and your friends would still be here, but I promised I'd return and I'm as good as my word."

"That's so kind of you," Cassie said. "The others aren't here at the moment, but I'm sure they'll be back soon."

"Not at all. Would you mind if I used the phone to call through to my pilot? I told him I would check in with him and let him know if I'd be awhile," he asked.

"Of course. It's in the kitchen," Cassie said, closing the door before she showed him the way, but as she turned around, she found herself staring at his back as he walked across the foyer towards the kitchen.

"Is everything okay?" Ravi asked as he entered the foyer.

Cassie waved him over, not wanting to be overheard. "I'm not sure. The guy who flew us here has shown up, which I thought was fine, only he asked to use the phone and he's gone into the kitchen—only I didn't tell him where it was. That's odd, right? And how did he know we were staying here? Or am I being paranoid?"

"I definitely think it's odd, but let's make sure." he replied, and he vanished before her eyes.

His powers might come in handy after all.

Cassie placed her hand on her head, which was throbbing again, and she wished that her healing powers extended to her own injuries. With a sigh, she was about to walk back to the living room when she heard a car hurtle up the driveway. Yanking open the door, relief washed over her as she watched all four of her friends spill out of the car, unharmed. Cassie ran out and threw her arms around Addie and Selene.

"I'm so relieved you're all okay! What happened back there? I'm so sorry I left you, I…" Cassie rambled.

"Don't apologize! Ravi did the right thing, pulling you both out of there," Addie reassured her. "But before we tell you what happened, you need to see this!" She held up the book so Cassie could see the old photograph of Sir Dirk Dillinger.

Cassie frowned as she looked from the book to her friends. "What is this?"

"Long story short, our rich jet-setter is also the creature that lured us to the ruins." Selene said.

"What?" Cassie gasped.

"Right? So the plot thickens..." Addie agreed.

"No. You don't understand. He's here!" Cassie hissed.

"What do you mean, here?" Marek asked.

"I mean here, as in the kitchen."

"Why did you let him in?" Selene asked.

"Why wouldn't I? He said he'd returned to see if we were still here and if we needed a flight home. How was I to know he wasn't who—or what—he said he was?" Cassie asked.

"Probably because this is Auberon..." Jove stated.

"Well, what are we going to do?" Cassie asked, looking over her shoulder into the house, hoping Ravi would appear beside her.

Chapter Three

Addie

They all jumped as Ravi appeared suddenly beside Cassie. "Hey! Glad you all are back. I'd like to say safe, but I'm not sure that's the case."

"Why, what did you hear?" Cassie asked.

"It didn't really make much sense, but I'm fairly certain the person he was talking to wasn't his pilot. There was no talk of leaving or anything like that. It was more confirmation that he was in the manor. I don't like it—I got the impression from the tone of his voice that his intentions aren't good." Ravi explained.

The others quickly filled him in on who his guest really was as they huddled together. Ravi swore under his breath.

"So how are we going to get rid of him without him knowing we suspect anything?" Selene whispered.

"I don't think we can." Marek said. "But we might be able to make the most of his visit."

"How?" Addie asked.

"Just follow my lead." Marek said, leading them back into the house. Addie and Jove walked in last, and Addie closed the door behind them, before turning around and accepting Jove's outstretched hand. As though on cue, Dirk strode towards them from the kitchen, his hands casually in his pockets as though he didn't have a care in the world. When he looked up, he didn't appear to be in the least bit surprised by the number of people now standing in the foyer.

"Thank you for that…" he said, before Marek thrust his hands outwards and froze the man in place.

"Uh, okay…" Cassie said. "Now what?"

"Now I want you to use your telekinesis abilities to raise him up off the ground." Marek instructed Cassie, who grinned, clearly excited at the opportunity to flex her powers. They all watched with anticipation as Dirk started rising into the air.

"Good. Now can you rotate him so he's horizontal?" Marek asked.

"Too easy." Cassie confirmed as she did what he asked.

"Addie," he turned to her, "I want you to use your clairvoyance and psychometry abilities to see into his mind. Hopefully, you'll be able to find out what he's doing here."

Addie nodded and, letting go of Jove's hand, walked over to the motionless intruder. Chewing on her lower lip, Addie hesitated, uncertain of how to proceed, aware of all the eyes on her. Deciding it would work best to try to pretend like they weren't there, Addie closed her eyes and placed her hands-on Dirk's head. Instantaneously, her mind flooded with horrific images that made her gasp, knocking the air out of her. She felt like she'd grasped hold of a live wire, unable to release it despite wanting to. Addie was vaguely aware of the voices of her friends, asking if she was okay, of them warning Jove not to touch her, but she was unable to pull back her mind from Dirk's. The rapid flickering of images started slowing, allowing Addie to catch more than just a glimpse of each one. She saw the creature in its true form, its rage almost knocking her backwards. Addie delved a little deeper into the image, trying to determine the cause of the anger. She was met with their faces—

or at least, the faces of the Auberon witches as he'd known them.

"He hates us—them—the Auberon witches," Addie spoke as the information came to her. "He's spent decades, longer even, trying to work out how it is they can come back again and again. The creature believes they are the source of the immortality he seeks." She paused as the images sped up again and Addie struggled to pin down a single memory or thought. It felt as though he knew she was in his head, that he was fighting against her intrusion somehow. Addie was determined to find out all that she could, and she closed her eyes, pressing her hands against his head a little more firmly. The images slowed right down, and Addie found herself looking at her home, as though she was facing it from the other side of the road. Frowning, she watched as her car pulled into the driveway.

"I can see myself! I'm at my house, getting out of my car. I'm walking towards the mailbox—there's a yellow envelope sticking out." Addie paused, suddenly remembering the day and what the image was about to show them. Taking a deep breath, she forced herself to keep speaking as the memory unfolded. "The envelope is only addressed to me, which I find strange. There's no return address on the back, and I'm opening it as I walk up the driveway towards the front door. I pull out the contents and my handbag and keys fall to the ground." Addie gasped; the pain as real as when she'd experienced it the first time around.

"Addie? What is it?" Jove asked, but his voice sounded far away.

"I... I'm holding a pile of photographs. Images of my husband. With his co-worker. The woman he was having an affair with. There are images of them together, in our bed, among other places. The worst one is of the two of them leaving a maternity clinic, smiling like they've just received the happiest news of their lives." Addie had to stop talking as a sob engulfed her. It was the day her life as she'd known it had crashed down around her. Not only was she confronted with the pain of her husband's infidelity, she was faced with the gut-wrenching reality that he was going to become a father: Something Addie had never been able to give him, despite all their best efforts. All she'd ever wanted was to surround herself with children, and now he was living that dream with someone else. Just when she thought she couldn't bear to see any more, the images changed.

"It looks like I'm now in an office. Though I'm quietly closing the door behind me so I don't think I'm supposed to be there. I'm sitting behind the desk and looking at a computer monitor, scrolling through files." Addie paused, frowning as she tried to make sense of what she was seeing.

"I'm opening a file with Selene's name on it!" Addie gasped. "There are test results—they're negative, but I'm conjuring up new results. These are positive." She paused as the images shifted again.

"Now I'm sitting behind the wheel of a car, gripping the steering wheel with both hands. The engine is running, but the car is stationary, as though I'm waiting for someone. Looking out the windshield, I can see I'm sitting at an intersection, it's quiet aside from my vehicle and a vehicle to my left. Their light changes from red to green and as they cross the intersection, my car speeds forward, my foot pressing the accelerator to the floor. Just before I plough into them, I see a male driver and two children in the back seat."

Addie felt strong hands pull her backwards by the shoulders and she collapsed to the ground. Opening her eyes, she realized her face was wet with tears as she brushed her cheeks with her fingertips.

"Addie? Are you okay?" Jove asked and she looked up, only now noticing he was beside her on the floor, cradling her in his lap. Addie blinked a couple of times, feeling disoriented and unable to answer. Turning her head to the side, she saw Cassie and Selene, both of them looking equally pale, their teary eyes wide with disbelief.

"I can see this is very upsetting to the three of you," Marek said gently, placing his hands on Selene's shoulders, "but can I ask you to talk me through it? I don't know that I understand what's just happened."

Addie shakily rose to her feet with the help of Jove. "It would appear that Larkin did more than just offer us a flight. He instigated the traumatic circumstances that led the three of us to be at that airport in the first place. According to his memories, he was the one who delivered the images to my house that led me to discover my husband's affair."

"And those test results were positive for breast cancer. He faked them to scare me, which led me to leave my life behind." Selene said softly, hugging herself.

"He…" Cassie's voice shook as a sob coursed through her. Ravi grabbed her hand with both of his, seemingly giving her the strength to continue. "He was the one who drove into my family's car, killing all three of them. They were just left there in the middle of the road while he drove off."

"This is unbelievable. This Larkin creature must have somehow found out who you were and brought you back together—all so he could find a way to your powers and make himself immortal?" Jove asked.

"But we're not immortal, are we? I mean, I know we've seen pictures of ourselves from the past, but they're not really us exactly. Are they? If we were immortal then how am I here now, when the warlock killed the last version of me in 1920?" Addie rambled, feeling like she was on the brink of hysteria.

"I know there is a lot to process, but right now, I don't know that we have the time. We need to find a way to get through that lock in the wall if we have any chance of fighting against what's coming for you." Marek said.

"Marek's right—standing here asking ourselves more questions won't get us anywhere. We need to find…" Ravi was cut off as they heard a strange muffled sound, and they turned to see Larkin starting to move.

"Quick! The freeze is wearing off!"

Chapter Four

Selene

Marek pulled Selene behind him as he stepped forward towards Larkin.

"Be careful!" Selene cried out as a deep guttural growl emanated from their inhuman enemy, straining against the powers that bound him.

Marek held his hands out to restrain him. "It's not going to be enough to keep freezing him, he'll break free, eventually."

"What else can we do with him?" Jove asked.

"We can't kill him—he might still have information we need!" Cassie exclaimed.

"I have an idea," Selene said, stepping out from behind Marek and approaching Larkin.

"Selene! What are you doing?" Marek reached for her hand but she pulled away.

"Trust me. I can be useful too," she replied as she edged as close as she dared. Larkin's eyes flew open and Selene jumped as the full intensity of his hatred was directed straight at her. A monstrous growl emanated from him, echoing around the foyer and sending a chill right through to her bones. Yet Selene was determined to be brave like her friends. Leaning down as close as she dared, Selene forced herself to hold his stare as she spoke.

"You are Larkin Frey, and you are powerless against us. From this moment you can no longer conjure a human appearance." She paused as the figure they'd known as Sir Dirk Dillinger melted away, leaving in its place the twisted and monstrous figure of the real Larkin Frey. His body looked like that of an old tree, all bulging knots and gnarled limbs.

"You can no longer conjure magic—for any purpose," Selene confirmed, as Larkin screamed and bucked, dangerously straining against Marek's magic as Selene stripped him of his ability to act against them. One arm broke free, and he thrust it towards her, managing to grab the material of her sleeve as she screeched and stumbled backwards.

"You're okay, I've got you," Marek said, grabbing her around the waist as she righted herself. "Go and open the doors through the kitchen that open out onto the garden."

Selene ran through the foyer and through the kitchen towards the glass doors. Pushing them open, she hurried through to the garden and stepped aside, not sure what she was waiting for.

The dark purple clouds now surrounded the manor, bursts of lightning shooting across them, and Selene was certain she could feel the electricity surging through the air. She looked up as the windows started trembling; looking through them, she saw Larkin floating across the kitchen towards her emitting an eerie, high-pitched shriek. On the other side of him were Cassie and Marek, their arms outstretched as Marek fought to keep the creature bound while Cassie used her magic to push it across the room and outside, the others following closely behind them. Selene bit her lip as she watched both of them strain with every stride as they pushed Larkin out into the open. Thunder rumbled loudly as they joined her outside, and Selene wondered if it was a good or a bad omen.

Cassie pushed Larkin into the middle of the garden, her knees buckling under the strain. Selene reached out, placing her hands on her back.

"Can I help?" she asked.

Cassie inhaled sharply, before steadily straightening her shaking legs. Cassie turned to her. "I think you just did. It's like your power is giving me strength."

"Addie! Quickly!" Selene called, and Addie hurried over and placed her hands on the other side of Cassie's back.

"On the count of three, I want you to focus your energies on me," Cassie demanded. She took a deep breath than started to count. As she called "three," she pulled her arms back and with a groan of exertion almost as loud as the thunder above, she shoved her hands forward and sent Larkin hurtling through the air, up over the trees surrounding the manor and into the storming clouds. The thunder subsided suddenly, as though the clouds themselves had inhaled.

"Uh, guys? Can you hear that?" Jove asked, stepping forward across the grass with his hand over his forehead as he looked up at the sky.

"What? Everything's gone quiet." Addie replied.

"It's too quiet." Ravi said.

"No, it's not. You can't hear that? It's like a high-pitched whistling sound," Jove said, lowering his hand and turning to face them. His face was contorted as though he was in pain and he suddenly clapped his hands over his ears and fell to his knees.

"Jove!" Addie cried as she hurried to his side. "What is it?"

"Wait!" Selene said. "I can hear it now, too!" One by one they looked up at the point in the clouds where they'd last seen Larkin, where the ominous sound now seemed to come from.

"Look!" Selene pointed up at the sky. The point where Larkin had disappeared was blackening, as though his poisonous nature was polluting the very sky.

"Oh, boy. I don't like the look of that…" Addie said as she helped Jove to his feet.

"I think we should get inside," Selene said, and without another word, they all followed her and lined up along the kitchen window to look out from the safety inside the manor. Selene reached out and grabbed

Marek's hand as they watched the blackness of the clouds expand across the sky while also rising further upwards. It seemed to draw in the lightning as it went until the bolts formed an enormous ball. The high-pitched sound increased until they all had to cover their ears.

"Get down!" Ravi yelled over the noise, and they all fell to the ground as there was a blinding flash of white light and a resounding boom that shook the entire manor. The windows above them shattered inwards, covering the group with shards of glass.

Selene lowered her hands from over her head and glanced at Marek. "Is it over?" He didn't reply, but cautiously got to his feet and leaned out from the gaping hole that had once been the window.

"Whatever that was, it's gone," he advised, as the others got to their feet and joined him.

"Those strange purple clouds haven't gone anywhere though," Selene said, wrapping her hands around Marek's arm. She looked up at his face, noting his clenched jaw and the worried look in his eyes.

"What is it?" she asked softly.

"I'm not sure. There's something off about those clouds, I just can't work out what it is," he replied.

"You mean aside from the fact they're purple?" Cassie scoffed.

"I feel like I've read something about this somewhere. I've been trying to remember since we first saw them back at my house," Marek explained.

"What about the books we brought back? Do you think there may be something about it in them?" Selene asked.

"It's a starting place," Marek said as he grabbed her hand and led her from the kitchen, the others stepping over the broken glass behind them.

Chapter Five

Cassie

About to follow her friends out of the kitchen, Cassie turned and looked back at the glass on the floor. With her head tilted to the side, she lifted her hands and watched the shards rise into the air. Smiling to herself, Cassie sent the pieces of glass towards the window frames and effortlessly put the panes back together before she turned and followed her friends into the living room.

"Why are you smiling?" Addie asked, looking up from where she sat on one of the lounges as Cassie entered.

"I just fixed the kitchen windows," Cassie admitted proudly.

"You have the coolest gift," Selene said wistfully from where she sat on the carpet beside Marek, effortlessly looking like a model about to have her photo taken.

"Excuse me, but who's the one with the ability to convince a bad-ass enemy that he's powerless against us?" Cassie asked as she walked over and sat beside Ravi on the opposite lounge.

Selene grinned. "Yeah I guess that was pretty cool."

"Obviously, I think you're wonderful," Marek said, planting a kiss on the side of Selene's head, "but we need to get to work. I might not know what those clouds mean, but while they're still hovering above us, I'm certain we're still in danger."

"You're right," Cassie said, grabbing another book from the pile and opening it up. They sat together in silence, each of them lost in the words before them. Though it wasn't long before Selene spoke up.

"I'm going through the book I started reading on the way over here—it looks like it was written by a Protector, though how long ago, I'm not sure. Anyway, it says here that the Auberon Witches re-enter the mortal realm every hundred years, but they're not born into it like the surrounding humans."

"Huh? What does that mean?" Cassie asked, marking her spot in her book with her finger while she looked up at Selene.

"I'm not sure. It says that, based on the observations of the Protectors over the centuries, the three witches—I guess that's us—reappear in the mortal realm as adults, as though they'd been there all along. They have no recollection of where they were, and in their minds, they believe they've been present in this realm all along. They believe they are just like any other mortal in this realm until they activate their powers and the truth of their nature is revealed to them…" Selene's voice trailed off as she turned and looked to Marek, the confusion on her face mirroring the way Cassie felt.

"So, what? We don't exist and then we do? Surely that's not possible," Addie said with a hint of alarm in her voice.

"I've come to believe that anything is possible," Cassie said softly, looking down at her hands. Her heart pounded in her chest.

How can someone not be here one second, and then be here the next?

"No, that can't be right," Addie said, getting to her feet, the skirt of her flared dress swishing against her knees. "We have pasts—in this life, that is. We were normal people before we met each other and came here.

We have our own history, our memories, our childhoods…"

Cassie frowned. "Yet as you say that, I'm trying to think back to when I was a child—and I can't." She covered her mouth with her hand.

"Me either!" Selene exclaimed.

Addie shook her head. "This is ridiculous, I know I was a child, and I grew up, and I went to school and had friends… but I can't seem to pin down an actual memory. Oh, my goodness…" She pressed her hand against her chest as she paced the room.

Jove got to his feet and went to her. "What is the earliest memory you can think of?"

Addie stopped pacing as she thought. "I… I'm not sure."

"How about you?" Ravi asked Cassie. She ran her fingertips over her lips as she strained her memory as far back as she could.

"I can remember walking along a path in a park. A dog came running up to me, his owner not far behind him. It was the day I met my husband—it was his dog that had escaped. I was 21," Cassie said in a hushed voice.

"Nothing before then?" Ravi asked.

Cassie shook her head and swallowed thickly. The whole concept was overwhelming and she felt as though she was on the brink of freaking out.

"Twenty-one," Selene said. "That seems to be the earliest memory I have too. My 21st birthday was when my parents introduced me to the man they intended to be my husband. But there were people there. Lots of people. How could I have had a birthday party if I'd just appeared out of nowhere?"

"Your guess is as good as mine, but I can't remember anything earlier than 21 either," Addie confessed.

"Ugh, this is making my head hurt," Selene declared, rubbing at her temples.

"Okay, this is obviously unnerving and I can't begin to understand how the three of you must feel, but can we come back to this later? I don't see that it helps us sort out our more immediate problems," Marek stated as he gently rubbed his hand over Selene's back.

Cassie nodded, grateful for someone stepping in and taking control of the situation. Her anxiety over her existence was subsiding with the renewed focus on the task at hand. "I think what we can take from this knowledge, is that it helped Larkin track us down. He knew when to look for us. What else have we got here?" She turned her attention back to the book before her, half paying attention to her friends settling back down and doing the same.

After a few moments, Cassie looked up at them excitedly. "I think I have something on the lock!"

"Hooray!" Selene exclaimed.

"What does it say?" Addie asked.

"It says the key to the lock will only work once a witch has harnessed the energies of their past selves and become one, once again." Cassie read.

"Great. Not helpful." Selene sighed. "How are we supposed to unlock the energies of our past? This is getting ridiculous." Selene groaned.

"Not necessarily." Cassie said, as she turned to look at Ravi. "I think this has already happened to me."

"What? When? How?" Addie asked, leaning forward.

"Well, after Ravi teleported us back from Marek's, I fell and hit my head on the box of photographs. While I was recovering on the couch, Ravi and I...uh...we kissed, and it was like...I don't even know how to explain it. An unlocking? But it's like the book said, everything, all my iterations as Cassie came back to me." Cassie explained.

"Why didn't you say something?" Selene asked, and Cassie felt guilty when she saw the hurt look in her friend's eyes.

"I had every intention of telling you guys, I guess it just slipped my mind with everything that happened with Dirk—I mean Larkin," Cassie apologized.

"Do you feel different? Or the same?" Addie asked.

Cassie looked up at the ceiling and pondered the question. "I think I feel the same, but I also feel different. It's a strange feeling, almost like I wasn't quite whole before and now I am. It also seems to have had an effect on my abilities too. When I was in the kitchen, I hardly had to think about picking all those shards of glass up off the ground and repairing the windows. It felt like my powers knew what I wanted to do before I did."

"But I'm confused. If it's a kiss that unlocks the memories, then how come Selene and I are still locked?" Addie asked.

"Excuse me, but…" Selene said.

"Oh, please. You can't tell me you and Marek weren't making out when you went with him to find the books." Addie said, using her fingers as quotation marks around the word books.

Selene blushed, causing Cassie and Addie to giggle.

"My thinking is, that because all of you are different, you each require a different lock to access your complete—archive—for lack of a better word." Marek suggested.

"That makes sense." Cassie said, getting to her feet. "However, the important thing is, according to this book, only one witch needs to experience this in order for the key to work."

Addie clapped her hand to her forehead. "Of course! Oh, my goodness!" She jumped to her feet while pulling the key out from where it lay protected under the bodice of her dress and pulled the chain over her head. Addie held it out to Cassie. "Try it."

Cassie hesitated. "Are you sure? I mean, the other Addie—you—gave it to, well, you?"

Addie shrugged. "We're in this together. I can't see how it matters who unlocks it, just so long as it happens."

"I agree with Addie." Selene declared as she let Marek help her to her feet. Together they walked around the back of the couch, where Cassie dragged the footstool to the front of the bookcase. Stepping up, she held the key tightly in her hand and reached up over the shelf, placing it in the lock. She turned and looked over her shoulder briefly. "Here goes nothing." Cassie closed her eyes and turned the key, gasping as she felt the lock mechanism click and shift. The wall started trembling as a purple light glimmered across it, and Cassie fell backwards off the stool and straight into the waiting arms of Ravi.

"You're not going to yell at me this time, are you?" he joked.

Cassie elbowed him playfully as she regained her balance, turning her attention back to the wall.

"It looks exactly how the wall looked outside before we saw the circle window appear!" Selene exclaimed.

Before their eyes, the shelves, and all the items that adorned them, started fading, quickly followed by the wall behind them. It didn't disappear completely, but became translucent, all except for the key which remained in the lock over their heads. They all lined up beside each other and tried to see what lay beyond the shelves.

"All that purple glimmering makes it hard to see…" Cassie murmured.

"I think it's another room—like a secret chamber?" Ravi said beside her.

Cassie stepped forward, her hand held outwards as she reached out for a book on the shelf. When her hand passed straight through it, only just visible on the other side, she turned and grinned. "Who wants to go first?"

Chapter Six

Addie

U h, well, since you've already stuck your arm in, how about you keep going?" Addie suggested.

"Sounds fair." Cassie stated.

"Wait. I'm coming with you." Ravi advised, reaching out and grabbing her free hand.

"I'm a big girl, I can look after myself." Cassie scoffed.

"And I love your independent self, however, since we cannot clearly see what's on the other side, I feel it would be reckless to enter on your own," Ravi replied.

Cassie grinned. "Well, come on then!" She dove into the wall, yanking Ravi in after her. A slight ripple spread out along the wall from the point of impact, a faint humming sound echoing with it. Addie nervously clasped her fingertips together and pressed them to her lips. Her instinct told her the other Addie wouldn't have given the key to her if it would put them in danger, but at the same time, she hadn't exactly had the chance to ask her about it. She turned to Jove. "What if I have it all wrong? What if the other Addie gave me the key because we're supposed to make sure it stays closed?"

"I'd say it's a little late either way." He draped his arm over her shoulder as though they were a couple relaxing before a sunset.

"Does nothing stress you out?" she asked, more in amazement than criticism.

Jove shrugged his shoulders. "Not usually. Where did stressing out ever get anyone?"

Addie raised her eyebrows and nodded, not able to criticize his logic.

"Okay, we're going in," Marek declared as he grabbed Selene's hand.

"Wait!" she protested, trying to pull him back. "Shouldn't we wait until the others return? You know, to let us know it's okay to cross?"

"Or we can live a little and find out for ourselves," Marek replied, raising Selene's hand and kissing it before turning and leading a wide-eyed Selene after him. The wall responded in the same way as before. Addie watched after them, unable to calm the nerves fluttering about in her stomach.

Why am I so hesitant? Usually Selene is the hesitant one, and Cassie is the brave one, and I'm in between. When did I become the scaredy-cat of the group?

"While we have a rare moment to ourselves, there's something I want to tell you," Jove said, keeping his eyes straight ahead, even when Addie turned and looked up at him.

"Okay," Addie confirmed, when he didn't continue.

Jove cleared his throat, as though suddenly nervous, and Addie frowned, wondering what could rattle his relaxed confidence.

"Jove? Is everything okay?" she asked.

He nodded, withdrawing his arm and turning her around to face him. "Earlier when you saw the memory of yourself through Larkin's eyes, you mentioned that you'd always wanted a family." His voice was soft and his blue eyes seemed to plead with her.

"I do. I mean, I did." Addie replied.

"Past tense? What changed?" he asked.

"Well, nothing, really. I'd love nothing more than to surround myself with children, but as it turns out I can't have any. Not even IVF helped." Addie gave him a rueful smile, trying to prevent herself from crying over a fact that was still so raw and painful. "I'm sorry. I'll understand if you don't want to be with me."

Jove frowned and tilted his head to the side as though he was confused. "Huh?"

"You know, if you want children, then you're wasting time with me…"

"What?" he said, before his eyes widened. "No! Shit, no, that's not what I was meaning at all." Jove grinned.

"So you're not breaking up with me? I mean, assuming you thought we were together. I know we've only been together a few days. It just feels… ah… crap…" Addie hid her face in her hands as she felt the hot flush of embarrassment rush up her neck and into her cheeks.

Jove laughed out aloud and pulled her against his chest. "Adamina Naya, I am mad for you! As mad for you as I was in the lives before this, and as mad as I will be in the lives to come."

Addie pulled back enough so she could look up at him. "I'm mad for you too."

"That's good to know." Jove planted a kiss on her forehead. "But what I was trying to tell you was: I'm a father."

Addie's eyes widened. "Are you serious?"

Jove nodded. "They're staying with my mother at the moment. When I first sensed that there was something going on around here, I knew there was a chance I could shift and I wanted to make sure they were safe. But yes, I have three children."

"Oh, my goodness!" Addie gasped and covered her mouth with her hands. "How old are they?"

"My eldest is my daughter, Skye. She's eleven going on twenty-one." Jove said, and Addie giggled.

"Then I have five-year-old twin boys: Raiden and Jorah."

"Oh, my goodness!" Addie exclaimed again; this time unable to stop the tears welling in her eyes.

"You said that already." Jove chuckled softly.

"I know. I'm sorry. I don't know what else to say." Addie apologized.

"Well, you could say that you would love to meet them. You could say that you could see yourself happy with us." Jove said, his eyes searching hers.

"Where is their mother?" Addie asked.

Jove lowered his gaze from her as a frown darkened his brow.

Addie could feel a wave of pain emanate from him and she held up her hand towards his head. "May I?" Jove nodded and Addie pressed her hands against his temples and closed her eyes.

Instantly, she saw him, sitting on a plastic chair in a stark white room, his head in his hands. Raising his head, he leaned back against the wall and Addie could see he'd been crying. He looked younger; there wasn't any sign of the stray greys that peppered his hair now. Yet, in his eyes, he looked exhausted. Spent. As though he had nothing left.

The image changed, and she saw him sitting beside a hospital bed, holding a woman's hand in both of his, his lips pressed against them as the tears streamed down his cheeks. The woman was beautiful despite her fragility, and her bald head was wrapped in a scarf the same color as her eyes. Addie could see she only had fleeting moments of her life left, and she pulled out of the memory, not wanting to violate that precious moment Jove had shared with his now-deceased wife.

"I am so sorry, Jove. Truly," Addie said as she withdrew her hands, placing them on his chest instead.

"I know. I am too. It's been a little over three years now, but she'll always be important to us, and I plan to make sure our children never forget her," Jove said.

"Of course," Addie replied softly.

"But you still haven't answered my question. Do you think you could be happy with my crazy little family?" Jove asked.

"Absolutely ecstatic," Addie replied as she reached up on her tiptoes and kissed him.

"Will you two hurry up and get your butts in here?" Cassie demanded, looking comical as her head protruded from the wall. Addie and Jove grinned sheepishly at each other, and with their hands clasped, they walked through the wall.

Chapter Seven

Selene

"I can honestly say I've never seen anything like this…" Selene murmured as she stared around the room. She hardly even registered as Addie and Jove finally joined them. The walls on either side of them reached ahead so far that she couldn't see the rear wall. While she couldn't see any light fixtures, the room was lit up around them as though soft sunlight was streaming through skylights. The walls were lined intermittently with shelves of magical objects and tomes, as well as framed portraits and photographs.

"It's like it was their magical den or something," Selene murmured.

"And by theirs, you mean ours," Cassie stated from the other side of the room as she grabbed an elaborate athame from off the shelf.

"Cassie! Put it back!" Selene yelped, startling Cassie so much that she almost dropped the knife.

"What? Why? These things belong to us now," Cassie countered.

Selene looked over to Addie. "Do they?"

Addie shrugged. "I guess so. Feels a little strange though, like we're intruding."

"Hmm…" Selene said as something caught her attention further down the room. She left the others as she walked towards it. As she neared, Selene could see it was a wooden lectern, its stand engraved with intricate symbols. Feeling instantly drawn to it, she ran her fingers over it and was almost knocked backwards by an invisible force. A strange sound came from her mouth, not quite a scream, but loud enough to alert the others who came running towards her.

"Selene!" Marek cried, spinning her around to face him. "What happened? Are you okay?" His expression was filled with concern, but Selene could only smile up at him.

Damn, he's a beautiful man. Can a man be beautiful? Because he is.

Selene turned her head to the side, admiring the objects lining the shelves—they seemed to have new life, a new vibrancy to them. She felt as though she was seeing everything for the first time.

"I think somebody just unlocked her full powers," Cassie said dramatically.

Selene just nodded as she grinned at them all.

"This is so not fair," Addie groaned.

"I'm sure yours won't be far away," Selene said, reaching out and giving her friend's arm a reassuring squeeze.

Addie gave a rueful smile and wandered away to look at something else, Jove trailing after her.

"What is this thing?" Cassie asked, admiring the podium.

"I think it's used to rest spell books on or something," Selene suggested.

"Yeah, I guess that makes sense," Cassie said as she ran her hand along the lectern's slanted top. Suddenly, a burst of light seemed to erupt upwards before forming a spinning orb of white and grey smoke.

"What did you do?" Selene gasped.

"Nothing!" Cassie said defensively as she quickly pulled her hands back. "I mean, I don't think I did anything!"

"What is that?" Addie breathed as she stepped up between the two of them.

"I have no idea..." Selene replied.

"Look!" Addie said, tapping their shoulders so they'd turn around. The men were all frozen in place, each of them looking over at them, unseeing. "They must have looked up when the light shot up."

"But how did they freeze?" Selene asked, feeling panicked.

"More importantly, how do we unfreeze them?" Addie asked.

"Worry not. We would never harm the allies of the Auberon Witches." A voice came from the orb, and the three of them spun around, their mouths agape. Selene nudged Cassie in the ribs.

"Say something," She whispered.

Cassie nudged her back. "You say something!"

"There is grave danger coming unlike anything the Auberon Witches have ever faced," the voice stated. It was neither male nor female, and every few words it sounded like there was more than one voice. The room trembled as a loud bang echoed from the manor side of the wall, as though punctuating the orb's point.

"The storm is intensifying. They are near," the voice said.

"Who are near?" Selene asked.

"You know who. You need not ask," said the voice.

"The Cult," whispered Cassie.

"Brenner," Addie murmured.

"While both have opposing goals, they both share the desire to kill you, and put an end to the Auberon Witches once and for all."

"Well, that's just awesome," Cassie stated.

"What about Larkin? Is he still a threat?" Selene asked.

"No. At least, not for your generation. For future generations of witches, we cannot say," the voice replied.

"We?" Addie asked.

"Yes," was all the voice said.

"Uh, okay…" Cassie replied. "So there are more than one of you. Who are you then?"

"We are you, and we are not you. We are what you once were, and what you will be. We exist—and we don't."

Cassie swore under her breath, unable to contain her frustration.

"I think what Cassie here means is that if danger is so near, what can we do to protect ourselves and defeat them?" Selene asked diplomatically.

"You already have everything you need to do both," the voice advised.

"Well, that's all well and good, but as I recall, that didn't help the last Addie when Brenner murdered her on the staircase," Addie said loudly.

The orb remained silent.

"Um, maybe you two made it angry?" Selene said in a hushed whisper.

"Ask and you shall receive," the orb said.

"Awesome. I ask that you get rid of The Cult and Brenner so we can live in peace." Cassie demanded. Once again the orb was silent in its reply. Cassie groaned with frustration and turned away.

Selene chewed on her lip, trying to think what to do.

Ask and you shall receive.

"Bring to us what we need to fight this battle," Selene stated as authoritatively as she could. The smoke within the orb swirled faster and faster as the room trembled.

"Selene, what did you do?" Cassie asked as she reached out and grabbed a hold of the lectern.

"It said ask, so I asked!" Selene yelped as she noticed objects had started flying off the shelves and hurtling towards them. She closed her eyes and threw her arms up over her face, expecting imminent impact, but instead she heard Cassie cheer.

"Now this is more like it!"

Slowly lowering her arms, Selene opened her eyes to find a series of objects hovering before her. Confused, she turned to look at what had made Cassie so excited, and saw her friend standing there with her arms held out from her sides while an invisible force appeared to equip her with a variety of magical tools.

"Guys! You have to try this! Just hold your arms out!" Cassie exclaimed.

Selene hesitantly stretched her arms out and screwed her face up as she turned her head away, expecting it to hurt. But as she felt something cloaked over her shoulders, Selene turned back around and stared in awe as object after object bound itself to her. The cloak was scarlet red and appeared to billow out around her, its hood down, resting against her back. Leather straps criss-crossed their way across her chest, with two others encircling her hips and her left thigh. Half a dozen cotton pouches, bound at their tops by golden string, attached themselves to her belt, while two athames, snug in their leather pouches, attached themselves to the straps across her chest, their hilts facing downwards. A third, slightly larger one, bound itself to the strap around her thigh where it rested against the outside of her leg. A woven crown of silver embedded with crystals rose before her, slowly lowering itself upon her head, and a wooden wand with quartz crystal points and engraved with ancient symbols hovered before her, waiting to be claimed. Selene reached out for it and clasped it in her hand. Her amazement was cut short as another thundering boom sounded from the manor, even louder than before.

"We are afraid you are out of time. They are coming for you," the orb spoke.

"Where?" Selene asked.

"They're running towards the manor from the ancient runes. Soon they will be here. You must fight. For all of us. They must not get your magic, or your lives." The orb dissipated and wisps of smoke drifted past them.

"What the hell?" Marek's voice came from behind them, and the women turned to find their men looking them up and down with bewildered expressions.

"Uh, we'll explain later. Right now we have to go— Brenner and The Cult are coming," Selene said. Marek looked down at the shelf beside him. "Can I bring this?" He pointed at a sword.

"Bring whatever you can. We're going to need it." Selene declared.

Chapter Eight

Cassie

Together they hurried from the hidden room, bursting into the manor as another thunderous clap shook the house. Cassie turned and looked behind her as the wall returned to its former state. The key shot out of the lock and fell to the carpet at their feet. Picking it up, Cassie handed it to Addie.

"I think you should look after this."

"Thank you." Addie smiled and took the key and its chain, carefully lifting it over her head so as not to dislodge her crown.

"Shit, will you look at that..." Ravi said. Cassie looked over to where he stood staring out the window and her mouth fell open. The unnatural purple clouds hung low in the sky, covering the tops of the tallest trees. Rapid lightning flashed through them, providing the only light, now that the sun could no longer be seen. Cassie swallowed thickly, her excitement over the secret room rapidly replaced with fear. Their situation suddenly felt very real.

"Can you feel that?" Marek said, looking at the ground.

"The ground's trembling..." Selene said softly. "Is it the thunder?"

Jove shook his head. "It's The Cult. They're closing in." With a rapid shudder, Jove fell to the ground, having changed into the fearsome wolf, ready to strike.

"How do we know what to do?" Addie asked as Marek led them from the living room, through the kitchen and outside.

"Trust your instinct." Cassie told her, clasping her friends' arm. "We've made it this far. I believe we can do anything together."

"You've changed your tune." Addie replied.

Cassie shrugged. "It was bound to happen." She released her friend and hurried over to where Ravi stood staring into the woods.

"I just wish I knew what we were up against," Ravi stated, holding a mace in one hand and a shield in another.

"Wait!" Addie declared, crouching down and placing the palms of her hands on the grass. Instantly she was blinded by a vision.

"I can see The Cult! Flames are spurting like fireworks out of the urn at the ruins, and as the embers fall, they're transforming into The Cult. The only weapons I can see are short swords, but that's not to say they don't have magic."

"How many are there?" Ravi asked over his shoulder.

"It's hard to tell. At least twenty, maybe more," Addie replied. "Oh, no… Brenner. He's right behind them and they're running towards the bridge."

"Stay in the vision!" Cassie demanded. "I'm going to try something." Closing her eyes, she held her hands out towards the trees, picturing the old bridge far across the other side. Her brows furrowed as she concentrated, directing all the power she could towards the bridge. "Tell me when The Cult are on the bridge."

"Now!" Addie called, and with a howl of exertion, Cassie directed all her magic towards the bridge, visualizing it breaking in two, sending The Cult toppling to their deaths.

"You did it!" Addie called.

"Did what?" Selene asked.

"Cassie just destroyed the bridge, sending most of The Cult down with it. About five or six have made it across." Addie said.

"Does that mean Brenner can't get across?" Selene asked, with hope in her voice evident.

"He's standing at the edge, looking across…" Addie said. "Goodness! He just leaped clear across it!"

"What kind of warlock is this guy?" Cassie grumbled, turning around to look at her friend just in time to see a bolt of lightning shoot down from the clouds and strike her friend.

"Addie!" They all dashed over, fearing the worst, but instead they found Addie sprawled on her back, looking up at the hovering clouds and smiling.

"I think I just reconnected," she said.

"Give us all a heart attack why don't you!" Cassie exclaimed as she helped Addie to her feet, while Jove nuzzled at Addie's legs.

"It's okay, I'm fine, really. But wow, right?" Addie said.

Jove turned towards the trees and crouched down low, uttering a deep growl as he bared his teeth.

"Looks like it couldn't have happened a moment too soon." Cassie said softly. They only had mere seconds to prepare themselves before The Cult burst through the trees, their short swords drawn high as they emitted an ear-piercing cry. Cassie almost felt sick due to her heart pumping so hard, yet the moment she saw the first of her enemies coming for her, it seemed that an old, ancient part of her kicked in, and she grabbed her sword from where it hung sheathed behind her back, hardly noticing its white glow as she swung it forward. Her cape swished around her as she spun gracefully, as though she was performing some elaborate battle dance, missing her opponents' blades as he thrust them towards her. Taking advantage of his momentary loss of balance, Cassie swung her sword back and drove it against his back, splitting him in two. With a hissing sound, her opponent dissipated into a cloud of black smoke, before being sucked up into the clouds above.

"Yes!" Cassie cried, raising her sword in the air. Upon realizing no one was paying any attention since they were fighting their own battles, she rolled her eyes and lowered her sword, preparing to fight again. To her surprise, no more Cult members came for her. As she looked around, one by one, her friends decimated their opponents until once again they were the only ones standing in the garden.

"That was too easy, right?" Cassie asked as Ravi came to her side.

"Speak for yourself," Addie groaned as she rubbed at her lower back.

"Where is Brenner?" Selene asked. "We know he was headed this way."

Before anyone could answer, a blasting hail came from somewhere within the woods and Cassie felt a chill run up her spine in spite of herself. "I think we're about to find out," she said. The group gathered together in a line, their anticipation palpable as they listened to the crunching and snapping of trees unfortunate enough to be in the warlock's path.

Come on, you bastard. Let's end this once and for all.

As the evil warlock stepped through the woods, Cassie felt a panic course through her; it was more intense than anything she'd ever experienced. Yet she forced herself to hold steady, taking comfort in the knowledge that her friends were there with her.

Brenner cut an intimidating figure as he stood before them, almost as tall as the trees themselves.

"Just remember, the bigger they are, the harder they fall," Ravi whispered in Cassie's ear and she gave a quick nod, but didn't look away.

"Well if it isn't the witches and their little pets…" Brenner's loud, booming voice, echoed around them.

Jove gave three sharp barks.

"You…" The warlock turned his attention to the wolf. "You're the one that cost me my witch in the cavern!" Brenner roared, bringing his hands forward as a fiery ball formed between them.

"You leave him alone!" Addie yelled, hurtling her spear towards the warlock where it lodged itself deep into his forearm, sending his fireball off course and hurtling towards the manor. There was a resonating boom as it hit an invisible barrier, splaying its energy across it before vanishing, harming nothing.

"Woah…" Cassie whispered, more to herself than anyone else.

Brenner cursed as he tried to grasp the spear with his large hands to yank it free. At that moment, Cassie felt the little pouches fixed to her waist belt warm against her thighs and she reached down and cupped one in her hand to see it glowing like her sword.

"Witches! Spell bags!" She cried, tearing the weapon from her belt and heaving it forward. It hit the warlock in the thick upper leg muscle where it disappeared, as though absorbed by evil. Within seconds, the area around where the pouch had vanished turned black and began smoking. Brenner howled, the spear in his arm forgotten as he fell to one knee, clutching his leg.

"Throw them all!" Cassie yelled and the three witches began hurtling their spell pouches towards the warlock. Seeing an opportunity to strike, Ravi and Marek sprinted towards him, weapons and shields at the ready. Jove ran ahead of them and launched himself at Brenner, locking his jaw on the exposed neck of the warlock as he looked down at his leg.

"Get off me, you mongrel!" Brenner hissed, grabbing Jove with his free hand and casting him aside like he was nothing more than a rag-doll.

"Jove!" Addie screamed when they heard the wolf's back make a sickening cracking noise as he hit a tree and reverted to his human form as he fell to the ground.

"Addie! Brenner first!" Cassie grabbed her friend's arm to stop her from running off, but Addie shrugged her off and ran to her love's side.

Cassie felt torn. She wanted to help them, but she also knew they had to kill Brenner if any of them were to be safe. She grabbed two more of her pouches and pegged them at their enemy, watching his skin blacken. "Aim for the black spots!" She commanded Ravi and Marek. They swung sword and mace at the smoking skin, and with each strike that landed against the warlock's body, it turned to stone. Realizing she was out of pouches, Cassie grabbed her sword and ran to join the men, but an ear-piercing cry came from her left and she turned to see Addie running towards Brenner, her second spear drawn over her shoulder.

"You killed him! You killed him!" Addie screamed, but before she could throw the spear, Brenner hurtled a fire ball that hit her on her shoulder, flipping her around as it sent her flying backwards. Her body thudded against the ground beside Jove's.

"Addie!" Cassie screamed, tears streaming down her face.

"Cassie! We need you!" Ravi yelled, and she forced herself to join back in the battle. She moved on auto pilot, taking pleasure in the way her sword reverberated every time it struck the warlock. The clouds above crackled and hissed like the sound of a fire as water is poured on it. Cassie stepped back and raised her sword to the sky, closing her eyes as she chanted at the clouds. With a magic far greater than The Cult's, the clouds obeyed her command and a torrent of rain cascaded upon them. Looking back at Brenner who was now on both knees, howling as his body was slowly but surely taken from his control, Ravi swung his mace at the warlock's remaining good hand, but Brenner caught the mace and lifted Ravi from the ground.

"Ravi!" Cassie called, running towards him, but as she looked on, the rain appeared to be compounding their magic and was slowly but surely turning the warlock to stone. Ravi let go of his end of the mace, landing on his feet as Cassie reached him.

"Look!" she said, pointing up at Brenner's hand as its fiery flesh turned to cold, grey, stone. Ravi grinned, gripping her hand and pulling her backwards. With his free hand, he put two fingers in his mouth and whistled to get the attention of Selene and Marek from where they had attacked around the other side of the warlock. They stepped back, watching in awe as their magic took a hold of their age-old enemy. As he thrust his head back and roared at the sky, his face slowly turned to stone, silencing him forever. The rain ceased, and panting, Cassie leaned against Ravi before remembering her injured friends. She dropped her sword to the ground as she ran to where Jove and Addie lay together on the grass. Cassie fell to her knees, the others close behind her as she leaned forward and checked both their pulses.

"They're alive!" Cassie cried.

"Oh my god…" Selene said as Cassie turned Addie's head to the side, revealing blistering skin down the side of her face, down her neck, and across her shoulder before running down her chest and left arm.

"Jove's back is broken in at least two places." Marek said softly.

"There must be something we can do to help them," Ravi said.

"Cassie! You healed Addie's ankle when she hurt it!" Selene exclaimed.

"That was just a sprained ankle! This is…this is far worse," Cassie replied.

"You have to try," Ravi said from where he crouched beside Jove. "Come on, Cassie. I believe in you."

"We all do, including Addie and Jove," Selene stated.

Cassie took a deep breath, taking one last look at her injured friends before she closed her eyes and held her hands out over Addie's body. She visualized the magic from the past swirling around her before it seeped into her and travelled through her body and down to her hands. She felt the warmth spread through her palms and across her fingers, and she willed the magic to heal Addie's burn. After a few moments, she opened her eyes and Addie groaned.

"It worked!" Selene cried, helping Addie as she tried to sit up.

"Jove!" Addie cried as she reached for him.

"It's okay—let Cassie help him," Selene advised as she held her friend back. Cassie shuffled over to Jove and repeated the same process until she heard him move.

"What happened? Is it over?" he asked as he sat up, perfectly healed.

"Oh, Jove!" Addie flung herself into his arms. He ran his fingers down the side of her scarred face.

"What happened? Are you okay?" he asked.

Addie nodded. "I was badly burned, but Cassie healed me. Unfortunately, I think I'm badly scarred."

"Wait!" Selene said and they all watched intently as Selene ran her hands over Addie's scarred skin, transforming her features to their original form.

"Thank you," Addie said, "both of you."

Getting to their feet, Cassie slipped her hand through Ravi's as they gathered before what remained of Brenner.

"What should we do with him? Just leave him here?" Addie asked.

"And have to look out at his monstrous form while we have our coffee every morning?" Cassie scoffed.

"I honestly don't have any suggestions," Marek said.

"I do," Cassie said with a grin as she let go of Ravi's hand and stepped forward. Raising her arms, she held her palms out to face the stone and sent long cracks along the facade. The long cracks split off into smaller cracks, then smaller still. "Marek, will you do the honors?"

"With pleasure." Standing beside her, he thrust his arms forward, decimating the warlock into hundreds of pieces of stone, and hurtling them upwards into the sky. As the stone hit the clouds, there were small bursts of fiery light, and as the last piece of Brenner disappeared, the clouds faded back to white and slowly drew back.

"And there he goes," Addie said, wrapping her arm around Cassie's waist.

"And here we stay," Selene said, hugging her from the other side.

Cassie nodded, smiling up at the clear blue sky, "…and here we stay."

The End

THANK YOU!

Thank you for reading this

WOMEN'S FANTASY FICTION BOXSET

THE AUBERON WITCHES
DESTINY SERIES

By Tara Weeks

We hope you enjoyed this book. Please consider
reviewing it on Amazon.

Your ratings and reviews help other readers to find and
enjoy my books!

ABOUT THE AUTHOR

Amazon bestselling author Tara Weeks is a natural-born storyteller who loves all things magic. She was hooked on Dracula early in her life and spread her wings from there.

Tara resides in the beautiful foothills of Oregon with her husband and two children. She loves hiking with her family, horseback riding in the hills, the smell of pine needles in the air and her faithful golden retriever Brik.

How does it get any better than this!

TARA WEEKS NEWSLETTER

Sign up for my Paranormal Women's Fiction newsletter on Facebook to get free book updates, giveaways and book promotion specials!

@taraweeksauthor

Printed in Great Britain
by Amazon